THE SHADOW RIDER

THE SHADOW RIDER

WILLIAM COLT MACDONALD

WHEELER
CHIVERS

This Large Print edition is published by Wheeler Publishing, Waterville, Maine, USA and by BBC Audiobooks Ltd, Bath, England.
Wheeler Publishing is an imprint of The Gale Group.
Wheeler is a trademark and used herein under license.

LIBRARY OF CONGRESS CATALOGING-IN-PUBLICATION DATA

MacDonald, William Colt, 1891–1968.
The shadow rider / by William Colt MacDonald.
p. cm. — (Wheeler Publishing large print western)
ISBN-13: 978-1-59722-641-7 (lg. print : pbk. : alk. paper)
ISBN-10: 1-59722-641-6 (lg. print : pbk. : alk. paper)
I. Title.
PS3525.A2122S53 2007
813'.52—dc22   2007028903

BRITISH LIBRARY CATALOGUING-IN-PUBLICATION DATA AVAILABLE

Published in 2007 in the U.S. by arrangement with
Golden West Literary Agency.
Published in 2008 in the U.K. by arrangement with
Golden West Literary Agency.

U.K. Hardcover: 978 1 405 64306 1 (Chivers Large Print)
U.K. Softcover: 978 1 405 64307 8 (Camden Large Print)

Printed in the United States of America on permanent paper
10 9 8 7 6 5 4 3 2 1

CONTENTS

1. The Gila Shadow

It was the third night after I had dodged the sheriff and his men when I found myself nearing Chili Joe's place. Frankly, I was pretty much up against it. I'd been pounding my saddle for more hours than I like to think about; my bronc was right close to being finished, too, though he hadn't been anything to get enthusiastic about when I got him. Howsomever, a man riding the outlaw trail can't be choosy, after he has had a horse shot from under him, and I'd had to take the first mount I could throw my kack on. Mister, I was plenty hungry; there hadn't been time to stop and get a decent meal anywhere. Besides, there were too many people ready and anxious to collect the reward offered for the capture, dead or alive, of the Gila Shadow.

You probably know Chili Joe's place. In case you don't it's about five miles southeast of Tia Lucia, down below the Mexican

7

border. It's a big square building, designed along the usual lines of Spanish architecture, with a courtyard, or patio, as it's known down that way. Built of adobe, of course, with a red-tiled roof and some strings of chili peppers hanging along the white walls for decorations. Probably, from the name, some folks might get the idea Chili Joe's was just another of those greasy dives seen along both sides of the border. To tell the truth, Joe didn't have much of a place to start with, but when tourists from the States commenced thronging across the line to Tia Lucia to gamble away their superfluous — and in some cases, hard-earned — cash, in the town's gambling houses, Chili Joe conceived the idea of erecting a high-grade roadhouse with entertainment for those who came to eat and drink.

The old-timers laughed when Chili Joe named his place the Golden Cactus. To them it would always be Chili Joe's joint, though I admit there was something to that cactus name: it was a good place to get stuck, if you had the gold, which same I didn't that night when I forked my weary bronc into the circle of light cast from the building windows. It must have been about nine o'clock in the evening. I was dog-tired, hungry, thirsty. And stony-broke. The place looked good to me at that moment, even while I realized I was taking a long chance. To a casual onlooker everything would have appeared quite modern — almost like in the United States — but just beyond that circle of light from the windows was Old Mexico and darkness. There anything could happen.

I reined my pony around one end of a long line of parked automobiles and over to a hitch rail that had stood there from the old days and which Chili Joe had refused to tear down when he put up his new place. For that matter, a good many of Joe's customers still arrived on horseback. I was pretty stiff when I climbed down from my saddle; I ached in every joint. There was a watering trough there and a small pile of hay. I did what was possible for my bronc, but I reckon he was almost too fagged to eat. I know how he felt all right; I sort of stumbled a couple of times while I was tending him.

Finally I drew a long breath and started for the entrance of the Golden Cactus. I noticed as I entered the front door and started on through to the patio where the tables were that a good many of Joe's guests were in evening clothes. Lots of pretty girls there too. It sure looked civilized, what with the lights around the walls and the white tablecloths and silver and so on. All those white shirt fronts sort of got me for a moment, when I realized how I looked. Dust was powdered thickly from the crown of my Stet hat down to my spurs. My corduroys and flannel shirt had been patched at one or two spots. There was a rip in my vest. The holster at my right hip was scarred and battle-worn.

Not that anyone would stop me from coming in. Tourists like to see the sights when they come across the border, and I knew I'd only be looked on as a bit of local color. Chili Joe encourages that sort of thing; I'd already noticed a scattering of cowmen about the room, and some of the pretty girls were certainly giving them the eye in no uncertain fashion. If I'd had the money to bet, right then, I'd have laid odds there'd be more than one love spot before the evening was finished.

I stopped at the entrance to the patio a moment. A Mexican string orchestra was making soft music, but I wasn't losing any time listening to it. Mostly I was looking the place over to see if it was safe to enter. That's an old habit of mine when stepping into places. In the center of the patio was a cleared space of hardwood flooring where the entertainers did their stuff. At each of the four sides were tables, nearly all occupied.

While I was glancing around for a vacant table my eyes fell on a couple of cowpunchers over in one corner. They looked me over when I came in, but that was all. I figured it was payday and they had come across the line to "eat Mex" for a change. Both of them were young, lean-jawed sons of the cow country, tough as rawhide, and tanned from years of riding — the sort a man likes to tie to when a ruckus is due to pile up. I was wishing right then that I had them siding me. A man gets lonely for friends, now and then, when most of his days are spent high-tailing it across country about two jumps ahead of a posse.

The music stopped, and as I started forward I noticed several people looking my way. Possibly some of them believed I was the genuine article, but the rest, more than likely, figured I'd been hired by Chili Joe to give his place a wild-and-woolly atmosphere. You know, Mexico, gun fighters, cowboys, bandits. That sort of thing. It's what tourists expect. What they don't realize is that Mexico has plenty of that stuff without it being faked.

A man and girl were just vacating a

near-by table, so I dropped down on one of the chairs. In a moment the string orchestra started another piece, and I was left to give my order to a waiter — in native peon costume — who had hurried up to take care of me. God! I was hungry. Nothing to eat at all the last couple of days and only a few sips of lukewarm water from my canteen. I took the menu the waiter offered and went right down the list. I guess that waiter thought I would never stop ordering.

I thought the food would never arrive, but I finally got started on the first dish. Maybe I gulped; I don't remember. Nor do I remember a meal that tasted better. Enchiladas, chili, tortillas, tamales. And a lot of other food besides. All tasty, steaming-hot, and high-flavored as the devil. I'm telling you, mister, I felt more like myself when I had that food under my belt and started to twist a smoke. That cigarette, by the way, emptied the last crumbs from my Durham sack. About that time the waiter shuffled up to learn if I wanted anything more. I did: *aguardiente.*

"Sí, señor."

Within a few minutes he returned carrying one of those heavy, squat stone flasks and a small glass. I was feeling a heap better now as I watched the liquor rippling out

12

of the thick-throated flask into my glass.

"*Nada.* Nothing," I replied to the waiter's next query, and he left me to my thoughts. At least there was nothing more *he* could do for me. I was wondering right then just how Chili Joe was going to take the news when he learned I didn't have a red cent in my pockets.

It's queer how a full stomach will change a man's attitude toward life. When I'd first entered the Golden Cactus I didn't care much what happened to me, just so I had a hot meal first. I'd figured the worst they could do was throw me out and beat me up. Or vice versa. I'd thought of jail too. That wouldn't be a new experience, anyway. But, like I say, a full stomach changes a man's mental attitude. I felt more independent now, strange as that may sound. In fact, I knew damned well I wasn't going to let anybody throw me out. And I didn't intend to be arrested. On the other hand, I wasn't going to get mixed into a shooting scrape if it could be helped. I simply had to keep out of the public eye as much as possible. What to do?

I didn't feel like appealing for help to a of the cowmen present, either. From point of view it wouldn't have been play the game. I'd gone into this thing opene

13

I'd needed food and I'd had it. It was my problem. Oh well, something would be sure to turn up; it always had, at least. I knew there was no use appealing to Chili Joe's better nature. He didn't have any. He was the type that wouldn't trust his own mother with a plugged peso. As long as things are rolling his way and the cash coming in, Joe's so affable he's fairly buttery-sweet. But once let him get an idea he's due to lose a few cents, he's a danged bad customer to deal with. Plumb mean, in fact.

I glanced around the room. At the moment Chili Joe was standing over in one corner, fat and greasy-faced with those long spiked mustaches of his. I knew he'd been watching me since I arrived. Maybe he suspected who I was, but I was right certain he wouldn't start trouble so long as I had money to pay for my meal — which same I didn't.

About that time one of these fandango girls came whirling out on the dance floor. You know the dance — a lot of stamping and tapping of red heels, whirring guitars and frilly skirts swishing in circles through the air. I figured I'd wait until the dance was over, then, when the orchestra started again, I'd just get out of my chair and walk through the door, hoping I wouldn't be

stopped. Only I knew I would. Still, I hoped. Y'see, I only had one cartridge left in my cylinder. My belt loops were plumb empty. Mebbe now you'll realize just how broke I was. You'll find plenty of waddies without food and drink, but seldom minus their ammunition.

And to top off all that, Chili Joe maintained a tough gang of hombres around the Golden Cactus — plenty tough, even if two or three I'd spotted did wear the soup-and-fish. And they were to take care of just such problems as the one I'd cooked up for myself. The more I thought about it, the more reluctant I became about that getting-up-and-stepping-off idea I'd been harboring. Not that I minded shooting my way out of the jamb — I figured I could dish it out as well as Chili Joe's gorillas — but I just didn't want to attract public attention in my direction. I hadn't forgotten that sheriff and his posse was due to catch up most any time.

The more I dwelt on the matter, the more convinced I became that another drink might aid in bringing a solution to the problem. I lifted one hand and signaled the waiter.

2. PASCAL SANTIAGO

So there I sat, sipping my second drink and making it last as long as possible. While I was trying to figure some way out of my difficulty a voice at my elbow suddenly made itself heard. The words were in Spanish, their owner asking if I'd mind his sitting at my table.

I replied in the same language and motioned to the chair across the table before I'd even had a chance to take stock of the man. Then as he sat down I gave him the once-over. I knew right then that something important was on the move. Don't ask why. Call it hunch, if you like, but I knew. When I'd entered the Golden Cactus this man had been sitting by himself at a side table, so I felt right certain he hadn't approached me just to pass the time of day.

Past middle age, he was, a big fellow, but there wasn't an ounce of superfluous flesh on his bones. His wavy shock of iron-gray hair didn't seem to make him look elderly either. I got the whole picture in my first glance: sort of a hawk-beak nose, thin lips, and piercing black eyes under shaggy gray brows; rather high cheekbones and a long powerful jaw. There was something dynamic about his whole getup. Life, vitality, power.

That's the impression I got. Somehow he reminded me of an old war eagle screeching to get into battle. I'm admitting I liked him from the first, even if I did feel he'd look more natural in cowpunch clothes with a hawg leg at his hip than in the smoothly fitting tuxedo he wore. He was Mexican, of course, or rather Spanish, as I learned later.

To open the conversation he drew from an inner pocket a small card which he passed across the table. On the card was engraved his name: Pascual de Hiñojosa y Santiago. Lots of this "big-Spanish-don" stuff here, I thought. There was something familiar about the name too.

"Well, Señor Pascual ——" I began.

"We'll dispense with so many words," he interrupted, a twinkle lighting his eyes for an instant. "At my home in the United States, where I now live, I am known as Pascal Santiago, Spanish gentleman of leisure, with some ranching interests."

It was all plain to me now. Pascal Santiago. He had come as a boy from his native Spain to the Argentine, built up an enormous beef herd down there, then sold out and moved to Mexico. For a time he had passed from the public eye, and when next heard of he was high in government favor at Mexico City. As I remembered it then, there had

17

been some scandal connected with the treasury department where he was concerned. I looked at him again. I'd have bet my last peso — if I'd had one — that Pascal Santiago was no thief. Anyway, he had dropped suddenly from the news and had been living in the United States these past several years.

"I don't happen to have a card, Señor Santiago," I began again, "but my name is ____"

Again he broke in on my words. "Wait, let me see if I can't tell you who you are." He pondered a moment or so, then, "You fit the description on the reward posters, señor — age, twenty-seven; six feet tall, reddish-brown hair, gray eyes, square jaw, weight about one seventy-five. . . . I wonder, señor, if you 'sling' a Colt gun as well as they say you do."

I matched his smile with one of my own. I wasn't worried greatly about what he might do. Surprised, yes. But not worried.

Here he switched the conversation to English, which he spoke as easily as his native Spanish. "I'm not far wrong then," he resumed, "in assuming you are Dale Stephens — otherwise known as the Gila Shadow, holdup man extraordinary, and badly wanted at present for robbing, in broad daylight, the Cashton Savings Bank. As one of the stockholders in that bank I'm wondering how you happen to be broke now, after making that cleanup at the Cashton."

"Suppose we say," I suggested coolly, "that the money is cached away where I can't get at it handy-like and that I didn't carry enough to see me through ——" I broke off, struck by a new thought: "Sa-ay, how do you know I'm broke? Not that I'm admitting that I am. . . ." My words went a bit lame at this point.

"You're broke, all right," Santiago said confidently. Amusement touched his next words. "It's easy to see. I knew the sheriff and his posse got a special permit to follow you across the border. It may interest you to know they're still looking for you down in Sonora. The sheriff wired the Cashton Bank this morning. A very neat bit of dodging on your part, Stephens."

I drew a long breath of relief. So I'd left that posse far to the rear. But I had to put up a front. I shrugged my shoulders. "Maybe it's lucky for them they're still down there," I said carelessly.

"Don't act stupid," Santiago said sharply. "You're not fooling me, and I don't think you're fooling yourself. You've got too much sense for that, I think. And you don't have to do any bluffing on my account. I don't much give a damn whether that sheriff catches you or not. I'm beyond worrying over trifles. I just passed on the information regarding the sheriff's whereabouts, thinking it might let you breathe easier." He smiled suddenly, and there was something mighty warming in that smile.

"All right, so I'm not fooling you." I grinned back. "But I am fooling that posse by being up here near the border. They won't think of trailing me up this way for two-three days yet. So maybe I haven't fooled myself either. But that doesn't explain how you knew I was broke." I knew there was no use denying that any longer.

"In the first place," Santiago commenced, "if you'd had money you'd have stopped at some little Mexican place and paid for your food. But you don't like to gyp poor folks out of money. And you won't beg. There was only one thing left: put on a bold front and come to the last place in the world that posse, or any other law authority, would expect to find you. Chili Joe has need of men like you, from time to time, so he appears friendly just so long as you can pay for what you get. Anyway, you've fooled Chili Joe. Of course there's always the

20

chance Joe might turn you up for the reward he'd get, but in that case he'd lay himself wide open to a raid some night from some of your friends."

"Which same I haven't got on this trail," I interposed a bit moodily.

"That," Santiago answered quietly, "is something to be determined later. Meanwhile, you came in here covered with alkali dust, so I knew you'd been riding hard. I could tell you were desperate from the amount of food you ordered. There was a general this-may-be-my-last-meal-but-it-will-be-a-good-one attitude in your manner. And you ate enough to satisfy three men. Now, no matter how hard pressed a man may be, he usually takes time to eat, if he has sufficient cash. Am I right?"

"Check," I conceded.

He nodded shortly. "How much do you need?"

Direct and to the point, that was Pascal Santiago. His offer came so suddenly, I could only blink for a few moments. Well, I'd been hoping for something to happen. And it had. Still, I hesitated. I didn't want to borrow money from a stranger — especially when I'd robbed a bank in which he was interested. At the same time I could see he'd feel offended if I didn't accept his offer. That's the way with those Spanish hombres.

"Ten pesos should cover it," I told him.

"Make it twenty." He laughed. "Tomorrow you may be hungry again." He drew the money from his wallet, placed it on the table, rose from the chair, and held out his hand. "I am very glad to have had an opportunity to help you, Señor Gila Shadow."

I took his hand but drew him back to the chair. "We might, Señor Santiago," I suggested, "have a drink together."

He nodded acceptance. I signaled the waiter to bring another glass. I noticed the fellow eying us rather strangely as he poured our aguardiente from the stone flask, but at the time I thought nothing of it. I paid my bill right then and told the waiter I wouldn't require anything more. The fact of the matter was I didn't want him hanging around our table. I wanted to do a little talking on my own account.

"¡*Salud!*" I proposed, raising my glass. "Your health, señor."

"*¡Salud!*" Santiago replied. We downed our drinks.

I went on a moment later: "Señor Santiago, thanking you is something that's understood. I'm in your debt. You've helped me out of a mean jam. It wasn't a dangerous position — yet — but it was damned awkward. If I can ever do anything to square matters, say the word. Right now I'm kicking myself for luck that made me pick a bank you were interested in."

"To me the bank is no longer important." Santiago shrugged his powerful shoulders. "And your thanks aren't necessary."

"They're sincere, at least," I told him. "I meant every word I said."

His eyes lighted a trifle. "*Bueno,* Señor Dale Stephens; I won't forget that. But I'm afraid there's nothing you can do to help me."

"Probably not," I admitted. Still, despite his words, I had a feeling he must have had some reason for coming across to my table. I wanted to know what it was. "Probably not," I repeated, "but I'd like to be sure. You are certain there is nothing I can do to square up with you?"

Santiago laughed softly as an older man might at a child. "Nothing at present, Señor Gila Shadow. You have your own troubles to attend."

"True enough. Just the same, I'm wondering a heap as to why you should take the time to come over here and pay for my meal."

To this day I've never gotten over thinking

about the man's cold nerve. Nine out of ten hombres in his shoes would have been frantic with fear. But not Pascal Santiago. There he was, laughing coolly and drinking and talking with me as though he hadn't a care in the world. What is more, he had taken the time to give my troubles a lot of consideration. Mister, I'd sure like to have that sort of control over my feelings.

Santiago didn't reply at once. He drew out a silver cigarette case, opened it, and extended it across the table. Usually I prefer "the makin's," but that pill wasn't half bad right then. If I'd only realized it, I needed that smoke to settle my nerves.

"The paying for your meal was nothing," Santiago said easily, with a careless wave of the hand. "Just put my actions down to the fact that I was trying to kill some time before I left here or that I gained a certain amount of pleasure from helping someone out at the last. Forget it. It's not worth mentioning."

Those words "at the last" sort of got to me. He hadn't emphasized them, but somehow they stood out like a clean brand on a cow critter, overshadowing everything else he said. In fact, they sounded for all the world like something a condemned man might utter shortly before an execution. I

24

didn't want to appear too inquisitive, yet by this time I was curious as the devil.

"Why kill time here?" I asked. "If you're ready to leave, why not just get up and step out?"

Again that soft, tolerant laugh of his, as though he were very amused at something I could not understand. Then he explained.

"That's just the rub, Señor Gila Shadow — I want to leave, and yet I'm not quite able to bring myself to the point of doing it. I admit frankly to a certain penchant for life. You see, the instant I step outside I'll be a dead man." He laughed again. "And I can't convince myself I'm ready to die yet."

Nerve? That man had courage, cold courage, if you know what I mean. Say, I was liking him more every minute.

3. Cartridges Wanted

My jaw must have dropped suddenly, because Santiago started to laugh at the amazement in my face. I tried to match his coolness, but I reckon I failed. I could feel my heart doing a trip-hammer dance against my ribs. Still, I managed to hold my voice steady as I told him, "That puts a different saddle on the horse. Howsomever, you seem to be riding easy — not fretting any."

"Nothing much to fret about," he replied. "Either my time has come, or it hasn't. If it has — well, I've often wondered exactly what lay ahead on the other side." His voice grew a bit wistful. "And yet, I'm not quite ready to go. I don't care so much for myself, but there are others to be considered. . . ." The words trailed off into uncertainties.

"It occurs to me," I commented as easily as possible, "that this isn't your night to shuffle off. We'll have to see what can be done about it."

Santiago shook his head. "I'm obliged to you, but we'd be outnumbered. You'd better keep out of my troubles and take care of your own skin."

"I don't see it that way. I always did have a craving for meddling in other folks' business. I've offered to help. Maybe we haven't a chance, but we can at least go out fighting." I paused a moment and added, "It's up to you."

Santiago considered a minute or so before saying slowly, "I'm half inclined to take you up on your proposition. Look, I'll make a deal with you: help me pull out of this tight spot, and I'll put five thousand dollars in your hand."

I just stared at him. Then he laughed. "¡Madre de Dios!" he exclaimed. "You don't

26

think that is the value I put on my poor carcass, do you? No! Five thousand happens to be all I have with me, at present. American dollars, mind you, not dobe ——"

"We'll forget the pay," I interrupted. "I wasn't thinking of that. Give me the layout and we'll spin a plan."

He nodded and commenced: "I won't take time to go into details. If I live after tonight you'll get the whole story tomorrow — providing *you're* still alive. Here are the necessary facts for the present. A few days ago I received a message to the effect that if I would come to Chili Joe's Golden Cactus I would get — for the sum of five thousand dollars — a piece of information I've been wanting badly. Now I learn that the whole thing was simply a ruse to trap me here where certain men can fill my body with lead."

"How'd you get wise to the facts?" I wanted to know.

"One of the waiters here is an old servant of mine," Santiago explained. "He overheard my prospective assassins laying plans and warned me. There's the story for the present anyway. The instant I leave this building and step outside I'm to be shot down."

Damned if he wasn't cool about it. I asked, "Who's due to do the shooting?"

"There are six men waiting in the tonneau of an open car outside," Santiago said. "They have a machine gun trained on the doorway, waiting for me to depart."

A machine gun! And me with a single cartridge in my forty-five. It looked like the odds were piling up. One chunk of forty-five lead against one of those stuttering death dealers! Nice thought, eh? I reckon my face did fall some, for Santiago said softly, with a bitter laugh, "I repeat señor, you had best forget me and look out for your own skin. The odds are too great."

"Not for the Gila Shadow," I boasted, and I wasn't feeling in a boasting mood right then, either. "Anyway, I need that five thousand you mentioned." Dammit! Those weren't the things I wanted to say at all. I wanted to tell him that I liked him a heap and that all the machine guns in the country couldn't stop me from lending a hand if it were physically possible. But, shucks, it's hard for one man to tell another those things.

I remembered noticing, now, as I had entered the Golden Cactus, that there had been a big open car drawn up near the entrance, with some sort of bulky object, covered with tarpaulin, in the rear seat. Six men waiting there too. Three that looked like they had come from north of the border line, and three were breeds of some mixed bloods. I hadn't paid much attention at the time. But now I was thinking about them a lot, and it came to me that even then they stood ready to yank off that tarpaulin covering and let loose that stuttering devil, when Santiago put in an appearance.

Gradually a plan was forming in my mind. "Have you got a car parked outside?" I asked next.

Santiago nodded. "An Hispano-Avispa model. The factory in Madrid guarantees it to do one-twenty an hour. I've never pushed it above ninety-five." He smiled. "Perhaps tonight is the right time to put it to the test."

"Ninety-five will be plenty," I assured him hastily.

"Can you drive an Hispano-Avispa?"

"I saw one once. I didn't figure anybody drove 'em. At the rate it was going I'd have bet money it flew of its own accord." I grinned at him. "Me, I never tried to drive anything but a fliv — and that time I hit a livery stable, head on, while I was still looking for the whipsocket. Nope, I'm not up on these big imported gas buggies, and I don't intend to try any driving. That's your part. You can make your getaway while I'm handling that machine-gun crew."

29

"Your score doesn't tally with mine," Santiago said stubbornly, and I knew right then I wasn't going to be able to change his mind. "If I leave, you leave with me. Otherwise the deal is off."

"All right," I consented. "I'll figure to pull out when you do, but I want you to have the engine running so there won't be any time wasted in getting started."

He saw that I had a plan and wanted to know what it was.

"When you see me leave the Golden Cactus," I told him, "you follow close on my heels. There's a couple of cow hands you can see across the room. See? Seated at that corner table? Yeah, they're the ones. I aim to talk them into helping us out. You'd better go back to your own table now. Don't pay your bill or give any sign of being ready to leave. There's no use advertising that you're about to slope out of here. It might even be a good idea to order some more food or drinks, just in case anybody is keeping cases on you. Let 'em think you're due to stay an hour or so more. Have you got a gun?"

"I've an automatic in my coat pocket."

"You can keep it," I told him. "I always figured an automatic would jam when you need it worst."

"The later models are greatly improved ——" he commenced.

"None of 'em are any good as far as I'm concerned tonight," I cut in. "I've got to get some cartridges for my forty-five. . . . You'd better be getting over to your table now."

As I look back, it seems queer to think of me giving him orders. I hadn't intended to be the road boss on this trail we were planning, but things just happened thataway. Santiago hadn't had any trouble understanding my plans, nor had he questioned 'em. I suppose by that time he was getting desperate — willing to take a chance on nearly anything that offered. But I still wonder how he could have had any confidence at all in a man with the reputation the Gila Shadow had tacked to him.

He rose from his chair. We shook hands again. He sauntered back to his table as though we had parted for the evening — or forever, for that matter. I finished my cigarette and shoved back my chair as though to leave. Suddenly, as if noticing them for the first time, I started toward the table occupied by the two cow-punchers I'd pointed out to Santiago. They spied me coming before I reached 'em.

"Howdy, stranger," one of them greeted. "Have a chair or a drink — or both."

The orchestra was swinging into the strains of *"El Sonoreño"* when I dropped into a vacant seat between the two and said I'd take both. I was glad of the music because I didn't want anyone to overhear what I was about to say. While both the cowboys at the table had been drinking fairly steadily, neither was drunk, nor anywhere near that condition. I could see they just had on a nice fighting edge, and I was tickled pink, if you catch my meaning.

"Name's Wilton," the tall blond cowpunch introduced himself, "mostly known as Rug."

"We call him Rug 'cause he's always layin' around," put in the other puncher, a dark-eyed hombre with an infectious grin.

Wilton went on with assumed dignity, "Don't pay any attention to this drunken sot with me. His name's Lamonte, but we call him Lamp 'cause he's always out when he's needed."

I laughed and shook hands with the pair. "Lamp, eh? Now I know why he's drinking that stuff that looks like kerosene."

Rug Wilton grinned. "Lamp always was a fiend for tequila. Me, I find pulque plenty strong enough, but when you travel with a souse you've got to drink the same ——"

"Who's a souse?" Lamp Lamonte demanded indignantly. "I've only had about five-six-seven-eight-nine drinks. I can still see plain enough to tell you there's a button off'n your vest."

"Look again, Lamp," Wilton advised, "and maybe you'll remember there aren't *any* buttons on it. Never was. The feller that cut this calfskin vest for me plumb forgot to make buttonholes, so I let it lay as is, always meaning to remedy the situation sometime, but never getting around to it. . . . Tequila, stranger?"

I nodded and realized it was time to introduce myself, at the same time wondering just how Lamonte and Wilton would take the news. My real name very few people knew, or if they'd ever heard it, it had soon slipped their memories. So I gave Wilton and Lamont something that would click right sudden: "I'm the Gila Shadow."

Lamonte choked; his eyes bulged. Suddenly he exploded, "My Gawd! The Gila Shadow!"

Rug Wilton took the news more calmly. "Shut up, Lamp," he said placidly, "until the gent gets through making *habla*. Anyway, you're not rich enough to interest him, nor me either, so there's no stick-up in the making. And you're no lily of the valley yourself, if it's purity you're thinking of!" Then to me, "I kind of thought I recognized you when you come over to our table. I happened to be in Cashton that day. I was standing right near the savings bank when you came tearing out with that sack of cash in your mitt, and you laughing like you'd played a big joke on somebody."

"You probably threw some lead at me too, eh?" I grinned. I saw Wilton didn't have his eye on any reward money, so I felt easier.

"Nope, I didn't shake any lead outten my barrel," he said, looking me straight in the eyes. I knew he was speaking the truth. "I figured there were enough hombres smoking your trail, 'thout I made the odds any worse. You weren't hurting me any — I didn't have any money in that bank — so it wasn't my business — and it isn't now," he added meaningly.

"Muchas Gracias," I thanked him. We swallowed our drinks

While I rolled a smoke with Lamp Lamonte's Durham, Rug said, "Calf roundup being over, Lamp and I calc'lated like we'd ramble around the country a mite for a vacation. We were punchin' for the 90-Bar, over near the Pecos, but when we pulled away with our pay in our pockets, we were plumb undecided where to head. I wanted to ride north, but Lamp, being a perverse critter, insisted on staying close to the border, so we arbitrated and stayed close to the border. Now that he's had his way, he's getting right restless. I can't figure whether it's the lack of honest crime or the liquor he's stowed away, but something has happened to him. He's craving action! Me, I'm plumb peaceful and was satisfied just to sit here ——"

"Yaah! You're peaceful, you are," Lamonte interrupted scornfully. "Who was it beat up them three greaser cops in Ciudad Juárez, just because they wouldn't let you bulldog that critter at the bullfight? I tell you, Shadow ——"

"Make it Stephens," I suggested. "Dale Stephens."

Lamonte nodded and went on, "I tell you, Stephens, this crazy pard of mine went right down into the ring before I could grab him. There wa'n't nothing to do but follow, so that's how come I was in the ring when it all happened. Rug already had his dewclaws on the bull's horns and was twistin' it down, when I notices a whole army of cops, picadors, matadors, toreadors, and every kind of 'dors' they have at them fights, getting ready to throw down on us — with mebbe the kitchen door, for all I know. The audience was so sore it was plumb bloodthirsty by this time, and I was interested in only one door — the door that led outside the ring. That's where I started for, dragging this nitwit with me, with him fightin' me off and insistin' on taking the toreador's sword for a souvenir."

"Souvenir, my eye," Rug grunted. "You'd a-took it, too, if it had been sticking in the fat part of your sit spot. I was just trying to pull it out. Lucky only the point stuck me. But that danged toreador didn't display much sense of discrimination when it come to exercising that darnin' needle of his. Me or the bull, one or t'other, it didn't 'pear to make much difference, just so he got to use it."

"Anyway," Lamp continued, "we got started for the exit door. We made good time too. Maybe the bull coming fast behind us had something to do with that. Howsomever, it didn't do him no good, 'cause we made that doorway in nothing flat for a record, passed through under the stands until we hit the street where our broncs was waiting, tied to a telegraph pole. There was three Mex cops standing there, just passing the time of day, or cursing their mothers-in-law, or something. If they got knocked down in our rush, it wa'n't our fault. They should have been patrolling a beat or tending to some regular duty. Instead they sure got indignant, and Rug commenced using his fists. Fact, he used 'em so fast, I didn't even get in one clean punch. Yaah!" he snorted dirisively. "You're peaceful, you are — not!"

"Anyway," Rug reminded meekly, "it was your idea to ride through town a couple of times before we pulled out, though. If you'd only listened to me we could have got clean away without the whole town chasing us and throwing things."

Lamp grinned with thorough enjoyment. "Gosh, it was plumb enjoyable. Some of the Mexes commenced pourin' lead in our direction, but we never stopped in one place long enough to furnish 'em a decent target — not until the soldiers was turned out to corral us. Gosh, it was sure worth it, the jail, the fine they slapped on us, and everything. Only that we'd known the *jefe* over in Tucson one time, we might have had some trouble."

One or two more stories were related. By that time I was certain Rug and Lamb were anything but peaceful. In fact, they were fair spoiling for a fight right then. That pair was looking better to me every minute.

I glanced across the tables to where Pascal Santiago was wading through a fresh supply of food, then turned back to my companions and broached the subject. "I'm thinking," I commenced, "that if I was to let out a sudden yelp for help my voice wouldn't have to carry far to find what I was looking for."

Both men sobered instantly. Rug looked serious. "We don't calc'late to go in on any stick-up games," he drawled. "But if you need any assistance sidetracking a certain posse, you can call on us."

"Us Americans got to stick together down here in *mañana* land," Lamp supplemented, "so shoot the wad."

I smiled. "It's not a stick-up this time, and I've already sideslipped that posse."

"Had an idea you were throwing a straight loop when you came over here." Rug nodded. "What can we do for you?"

I reached down and lifted my Colt gun out of its holster, then under cover of the table top extracted my lone forty-five cartridge and placed it before them on the cloth. The gun I left on my lap.

"I'm needing," I explained, "a few rounds to match that cartridge. Can you hombres supply 'em?"

4. THE RUCKUS STARTS

Both men looked disappointed. I could see they'd been expecting something entailing more action. "Shucks!" Lamp grumbled. "I was hoping you'd have some excitement to offer."

"Maybe I will," I replied. "Do I get some loads?"

Rug nodded. "Sure, we'll let you have all the ca'tridges you need ———"

"Wait," I cut in, "I'm out to buy your ammunition."

"You ain't buying from us," Rug said in hurt tones. "We'll donate what you want."

"Listen to me first," I told them. "I'm buying the cartridges and I'm paying a right good price. As a matter of fact, I've got two thirds of five thousand bucks to spend on ammunition. Are you interested?"

Lamp brightened, sensing action in the atmosphere. "Gosh, Rug" — he grinned — "it ain't going to rain after all."

Rug wasn't smiling, but he was a heap interested now. He looked me straight in the eyes. "Meaning," he said softly, "that such lead as you buy has to be delivered personal?"

I nodded. "Exactly — right out of the muzzles of your hawg legs. Such lead as I want for myself I'll just borrow."

"While you're borrowing," Rug suggested, "we'll appreciate being guided over the trail so we'll know just where we're headed. In short, what have we got to do to earn that two thirds of five thousand bucks?"

Both men donated a handful of forty-five cartridges. I loaded up under the table while I talked and shoved the rest into my pocket. "There's a hombre in here," I explained, "who's due to take a long ride unless we can save him from the trip. He's a square shooter and needs help bad. He's offered me five thousand to help him stay alive. I can't work it alone. I need help. We'll split the five thousand three ways if you want a hand in the game."

I gave them brief details regarding the rest of the setup and concluded, "So you see, while I don't know just why they want Santiago's hide, I figure him as straight and the right kind of a hombre to side in this ruckus. Are you with me?"

There was an unholy look of joy in Lamp's eyes as he replied, "Just try to keep us out of the fracas now."

Rug nodded. "We should be thanking you for the invite, Stephens. We'd commenced to get in a rut." He glanced across at Santiago. "So that's Pascal Santiago, eh? I've seen his picture in papers now and then and heard a lot about him."

"There's just one thing I forgot to tell you boys," I went on. "This gang that's all set to finish Santiago has got a machine gun set up in the back of their car. Are you still with me?"

Neither blinked an eye at the news. Lamp said solemnly, "I always did have a hankerin' to match my thumb against one of them things."

Rug chuckled. "They'll wish they had a coupla cannons before we get through with 'em. Cripes! What's one machine gun?"

"Don't be too confident," I warned them. "It may turn out we won't be able to make our getaway. If we do — and we'll have to be plumb lucky — it'll be in Santiago's car. There'll be no time to get horses."

"Ain't got no horses," Rug said. "Our broncs were sort of fagged, so we left 'em in a livery at that town just this side of the border. We come out here in that autobus that runs every hour. Hell of a rough ride too."

"I'm betting it will be rougher going back," I said meaningly. "Providing we get to go back. I've got a horse outside — mebbe I'd better call him a crowbait — but I'm not frettin' about leavin' him. My own bronc was shot from under me, and I had to hide in the brush a couple of days until the hombre that threw the lead gave up the hunt. I need a new saddle anyway."

Rug asked, "When do we start?"

"Right now, if you're ready," I answered.

Lamp beckoned their waiter and paid the score. While he was busy I leaned over to Rug. "You were saying you called Lamonte Lamp because he was always out when needed. Is that due to apply in the present instance?"

"Not none." Rug grinned. "I should have explained that Lamp burns brightest in a ruckus — burns lead and flame faster'n any man I ever saw."

"Except yourself," Lamp put in, catching the tail end of Rug's words.

The setup was looking better to me all the time. We talked a few minutes longer, then rose to our feet, and started out. I knew hell was about to break loose within the next few minutes, and I'm admitting frank that my mouth tasted sort of dry and parched. I glanced at Rug and Lamp. They were indulging in some sort of horseplay and laughing a lot. Damned if I didn't envy nerve like that. It sort of stiffened my own spine, so I guess we all looked steady enough as we sauntered past Santiago's table. He gave me a smile — with his eyes — when I went by, nothing more, but I knew he was ready to move.

Yeah, I was scared, all right. Me, I don't

like machine guns. We crossed the patio, Lamp on one side of me, Rug on the other. Reaching the front entrance, we paused in the doorway just a few moments to look the ground over. Yes, that machine-gun crew was still waiting, ready for action — two standing on the running board, two at the gun, and two seated in the front seat of the car, all ready to move the instant they'd blasted down Santiago. A few yards farther on I saw Santiago's Hispano-Avispa. It was a touring model, finished in blue and silver colors with a lot of nickel-plate work. The hood of the car looked a mile long from where I viewed it, and I knew there was plenty of power stored up there, rarin' to go places.

I spoke low-voiced to my companions, "C'mon," and headed straight for the machine-gun car, with the eyes of that murdering crew watching us close. Fact is, they'd looked at us a trifle suspiciously the instant we appeared in the entrance way of the Golden Cactus. Santiago would be coming right behind us, so I knew we didn't have too much time to waste.

As I approached the machine-gun car one of the men on the running board dropped one hand to his pocket as I neared him. Probably reaching for his automatic. I couldn't be sure. I noticed that three of the men were in puncher attire, with coats on and big sombreros pulled low on their heads. The other three were just plain border scum in civilian clothing. Something of satisfaction entered my heart at the very thought of putting this gang out of business — or at least foiling their plans. I'd walked a trifle ahead of Rug and Lamp by this time, though they were close behind, for which I was thankful.

The man on the running board who had put his hand in his pocket hadn't pulled his gun yet, though I knew he was suspicious of our actions. I closed in on him and asked calmly, "Have you got a match, pardner?"

He eyed me narrowly a moment, then growled sullenly, "No, I ain't. And I ain't expecting to have none, either." From me his eyes slipped back toward the entrance of the Golden Cactus where he was expecting Santiago to appear. I wanted to hold his attention and that of his companions a few moments more if possible. I gave him a sort of nasty laugh and sneered, "And if you did have one you wouldn't give it to me, would you?"

"Say, you," he commenced belligerently, "if you're lookin' for trouble ——" He paused suddenly.

I didn't dare look behind me, but Santiago must have appeared at that moment. From the men in the tonneau of the car came quick, snarling words, and the tarpaulin was yanked off the machine gun.

Right then Rug Wilton got in his work, and the ruckus started off with a wagonload of excitement. The machine gun had already stuttered out a handful of lead that must have missed Santiago when Rug leaped, with one bound, into the back of the car, knocking the murderous machine on its side! A hail of lead tore into the back cushion as Rug closed with the two men. Luckily Rug hadn't given those brutes time to train their aim on Santiago, though those first bullets must have swept dangerously close as he ran past us and headed in the direction of the Hispano-Avispa.

Six-shooters were popping like mad now. My own gun was out, doing its share. The two men in front of me went down like limp sacks of wheat. Lamp Lamonte was throw ing lead at the men in the driver's seat. saw one of them slump forward at th wheel, but the other managed to get his g into action. Lamp stumbled and went cra ing to the earth — no, by God — he was again, a long stream of flame and sm running from his right hand.

About that time there came the sudden roar of a motor. Santiago had gained the Hispano-Avispa in safety. That much, at least, we'd accomplished. From the corner of my eye I saw the long blue-and-silver car back out, stop, wheel around, and dash up to us.

"Drop it and come on," Santiago yelled, reminding me more than ever of some old war eagle, his voice coming strong above the roaring of the guns.

Up in the tonneau of the other car Rug Wilton hadn't been able to get his own gun into play, and he was struggling with the two machine-gun operators to keep them from righting their gun and turning loose with it again. Those hombres were plenty tough, and Rug had his hands full.

Understand, these things weren't happening just in the order I'm telling them. Everything happened at once. I'm surprised now at the way events stand out so clearly in my mind. At that time it was all a fast-moving blur of hot lead and smoke and blood. There was a lot of shouting going on, and in the door of the Golden Cactus I caught a glimpse of a group of frightened faces above white shirt fronts. Chili Joe's voice cut through the din once or twice, but I'm danged if I know what he was saying.

"*¡Poder de Dios!* Will you come?" Santiago's pleading tones carried above the noise of the melee.

I caught a frantic note in the words and realized something else was up. Yells sounded from behind the Golden Cactus. There weren't just six assassins after Santiago's hide; the gang had a few more in reserve. The motor of the big car was roaring like mad now, but it seemed as though we'd never reach it. My two men were accounted for. Lamp had taken care of his pair, but I saw he was down in the dust now, his body lifted on one bracing hand.

Through the ruckus I caught Rug Wilton's fierce laugh as he and his two cursing opponents struggled and bumped in the tonneau of the machine-gun car. The thought came to me then that that fighting fool would laugh on his own deathbed. I saw Rug's clenched fist shoot out and land on the head of one of his assailants. By that time something else was happening, and I didn't have time to see his next move.

From beyond the end of the line of parked automobiles, not fifty yards distant, came a running knot of seven or eight men. As they approached I caught the glint of moving light on steel. Reaching up, I snapped the barrel of my forty-five hard against the head of Rug's nearest opponent, then spun around and sprinted to help Lamp.

Lamp was down when I reached him. "Don't be a damned fool," he muttered through clenched teeth as I bent above his body. "You slope out of here while you got the chance. I'll be all right."

"Shut your trap," I gasped, half choked by motor exhaust and the sting of powder smoke in my nostrils. "Come on, we're fanning our tails out of here."

Jerking him to his feet, I half carried, half walked him to the Hispano-Avispa and lifted him over the side of the back seat. My gun wasn't idle on the way, either. At least, it stopped the advance of the new forces running to their comrades' assistance. Where they stood I could see bright crimson lances of flame leaping through the darkness. Lead whined all around us and kicked up gravel at our feet. Even as I flung Lamp into the rear seat of the Hispano-Avispa I saw Rug swing one final punch and come leaping toward us.

The next instant all three of us were in the car, and Santiago tramped down hard on the accelerator. Like a bronc under a sudden spur the Hispano-Avispa leaped into motion. No clashing of gears there, either. Santiago went from speed to higher speed in one smooth movement, and we were away on a long stretch of road, the wind tearing past in a mad rush.

Behind came the sharp barking of six-shooters, then the abrupt savage roar of another car being started. We were in for a chase, and I knew the fight wasn't over yet by a long shot! Apparently only a miracle could save Santiago from the murderers who were after his scalp, and me, well, I never did consider myself any miracle worker. It looked bad, if you catch what I mean.

5. RIDIN' THROUGH

Anyway, there we were, with the first part of our attempt successful. Rug and Lamp were in the rear seat. I was up front with Santiago. The Hispano-Avispa was just touching the high spots along that bumpy, rock-strewn road. I watched the speedometer go from fifty-five to sixty and on up to eighty. Me, I'm not used to traveling that fast, but when Santiago switched off the headlights the sensation was — cripes! I'll leave it to your imagination.

"They'll probably telephone ahead," Santiago explained as the motor steadied down to a long, smooth purr. "There's a small outpost of Federals up ahead, you know. We don't want to be stopped."

Maybe you can guess my astonishment at his calm tones. Dammit! The man didn't have any nerves. Every moment I expected that big Hispano-Avispa to lurch off the road and pile us up against a heap of rocks. "Aren't we going to Tia Lucia?" I gasped.

Santiago spoke just loud enough for his voice to carry about the sound of the car. "By this time they'll have telephoned Tia Lucia to be on the lookout for us. We'd be met at the outskirts. No, the only thing we have to fear now is getting past the soldiers on this road I've taken. Once past the soldiers and over the line and we're safe." He chuckled. "A very enjoyable little party, *amigo.* I felt you had the necessary nerve to put it across. How is the man who was hit?"

I was sure ashamed of myself for a minute. We'd been traveling so fast and I'd been doing so much worrying about my own skin that I'd plumb forgotten about Lamp. But then we'd only been on the road a few minutes or so — maybe a little longer. I turned back to Rug. "Is he hit bad, cowboy?"

Rug's words were reassuring: "Flesh wound in the hip; that's all. But we're both of us due to pass out from sheer fright if we don't get down from this cyclone we're riding."

Then came Lamp's voice, and I noticed he was sitting up now. "Sure, I'm all right. The bullet just sort of paralyzed a nerve for a few seconds or so. But I'm feeling like Rug — wound or no wound, I'd sooner walk than be flung through the atmosphere at this rate. Is Santiago still holding the reins, or did this blasted car run away from him?"

Just then the Hsipano-Avispa careened sickeningly. I thought we were sure as hell due to turn over, but Santiago straightened it out and we tore on. At that my heart was doing a hula-hula up in my throat someplace.

"Almost, I missed that curve," Santiago was explaining, and his voice was so damned steady it irritated me. Not only steady, either; I thought I caught a slight touch of amusement in his tones, and it sure griped me. He knew I was scared, all right, and I'm not ashamed to admit it. Right then I was thinking, Mister, I'd like to get you up on the hurricane deck of a wild broomtail someday and see how you feel. It might not be so blasted funny. But I didn't say anything — just hung on like grim death and watched the hills flash past in the darkness.

A lot of the time I kept my eyes shut; I didn't want to see the end when it came.

Back in the rear seat Rug and Lamp weren't saying much, but I knew they were as nervous as I was. I glanced past them along the road we had covered and could just make out twin pin points of yellow light still coming on our trail. I couldn't hear anything, due to the noise of our own motor, but I knew the chase was on in deadly earnest. Luckily the other machine didn't appear to be gaining anything on us; it wasn't losing any ground, either.

I mentioned that fact to Santiago. Right off I cursed myself for a fool and wished I'd kept my mouth shut: he just nodded and commenced feeding more gas to the Hispano-Avispa. Speed! That's no name for it. I was glad none of us were Indians just then. It wouldn't have needed more than a couple of feathers for us to be flying! After a time I risked another look back of us. The twin headlights to our rear had disappeared. Whether we had left them behind or they were the other side of a curve in a road, I didn't know.

Santiago said, "Can you still see them?"

I just grunted. I didn't want to commit myself in any way for fear he'd add another burst of speed. We rolled on without talking for five minutes more, then just to prove I was calm as he was I tried to make conversation: "Where we heading?"

His voice came back above the roar of the motor: "I'm taking the same road I used coming down to the Golden Cactus. There'll be soldiers up ahead, but if we can get past them we'll be safe, clear through to the Mexican border. It's a longer route, but it's safer, even if this road is rather rough."

"Rather rough," I repeated indignantly. "Road? Cripes! I thought those bumps we've been hitting were mountain peaks."

Again that irritating, cool chuckle. "You'll forget the road by the time we've come up with the soldiers."

"Why worry about soldiers?" I asked dumbly. "Can't we just stop and explain that you're escaping from a bunch of murderers?"

"Exactly what I don't want to do," he explained. "They've probably telephoned on to the post that I'm a revolutionist ——"

"Are you?" I interrupted.

"I am not," came his definitive reply, "but they'd hold Pascal Santiago on a mighty slim excuse. No, they want me for something else. I'm not safe in Mexico; that's all. . . . The soldiers are about four miles ahead, now, if I'm not mistaken."

And then it happened. I nearly jumped out of my seat — or was thrown out almost — as we hit a chuckhole in the road and one of the tires let go! Santiago clipped off the gas, wrenched the steering wheel around, and slammed on the brakes. I'll bet you could have heard the protesting shrieks of those brakes for miles. We rocked to a stop, right side up.

"Seems like we've slowed down," came Rug's voice, and I could detect the note of relief in his words.

"Blowout," Santiago said tersely. He swore a cool Spanish oath, opened the door on his side, and stepped out of the car.

To make matters worse, I could hear now, through the still night air, the roar of the pursuing motor, still far behind though. However, at the rate they were traveling it wouldn't take long to catch up.

Santiago heard them too. He said quietly, "You'll have to hold them off, amigos, while I change this tire."

Rug Wilton and Lamp were already out of the car. The earth felt good to me when I stepped out. Santiago rummaged under the rear seat for tools. I was wishing it was light about that time and for a few minutes I got my wish: the moon passed from under a cloud, and we were able to see around us.

Santiago had stopped the car in a narrow pass between two hills, the steep sides of which were studded sparsely with piñion, scrub oak, and mesquite. There wasn't much small brush, though, except a scattering of prickly-pear clumps; mostly those two hillsides were carpeted with chunks of broken rock of all sizes and shapes.

The roar of the pursuing car grew louder as Santiago worked. In another instant I caught sight of those twin points of yellow light again, twisting and weaving along the uneven road, but making good time nevertheless. It sure looked like we were caught for fair this time. Well, there's nothing like the feel of the old Colt gun in a feller's fist when he's in a tight. I spoke swiftly to Rug.

Rug caught my words and nodded agreement. We turned and ran about fifty yards back along the road, in the direction of the approaching car that was following us. Lamp stayed with the Hispano-Avispa, a couple of bandannas knotted about the wound in his thigh, to render as much assistance as possible to Santiago.

"Me, I'd sooner stay behind anyway and shoot it out," Rug panted as he ran at my side, "than get in that thunderbolt wagon again."

Lord only knows just what Rug and I

expected to do. We hadn't any definite plan in mind beyond stopping Santiago's would-be assassins. Our guns were out, but we knew we'd be outnumbered. Back of us we could hear Santiago talking coolly — once he laughed — as though this were all in the day's work. I could hear the clank of tools, too, so I knew he wasn't wasting any time.

About then Rug had an inspiration. "See that pile of rock up there, Stephens?" he asked.

I shot a glance up the rockstrewn slope where he was pointing. Then I got his idea. There was one huge rock up there, perched just at the edge of an outjutting shelf. What I noticed most was the heaped-up pile of boulders stacked back of it. That one big rock seemed to be the lone obstacle that kept the boulders from tumbling down the slope, heaped as they were, one on top of another.

Maybe you've been around a lumber camp sometime and seen a big jam occur when the logs are being floated down a river. Sometimes that jam is caused by one big log entangling the others in such a way as to halt the whole run. Then it's necessary to loosen that one "key" log in order to release the other logs before they can float on down the stream. Well, this was something of the same proposition. That huge rock was the "key" rock. Start it moving and the other rocks would move too.

At first I was inclined to laugh at Rug's idea. Not that it wasn't a good one if we could get that big rock loosened — but that big rock was looming up like the rock of Gibraltar. Lord! If we could only get it moving. I've known 'em like that before though, just a touch necessary to unsettle the balance Nature has maintained for years. The more I looked at that big rock, the more I wondered what had held it in place this long. There didn't seem to be any other rocks or any great amount of earth blocking it.

Even while I'd been considering the matter I'd been clawing my way up that steep hillside, with Rug at my heels. I heard him swear once. He'd tripped and fallen. Then as he gained his feet again he started to laugh.

"Look what spilled me," he said.

I looked. It was just what we needed. A broken-off tree limb had caught his toe. It wasn't big and it didn't look any too stout — half rotten probably — but it was better than nothing — providing we had the strength to use it.

The noise of the pursuing motor was louder now as we reached that big rock and started to work. Rug inserted the tree limb underneath, and we both lifted until I thought I'd pull my heart loose. Suddenly I got the surprise of my life. The rock had actually moved!

"It's ready to go," Rug panted. "Probably the next rain would have started it moving. Come on, give it the works!"

I could feel perspiration starting out of my forehead as we strained at that limb. Again the rock moved a trifle — and the limb broke in our hands!

"Hell's bells!" Rug cursed. "We'd had it in another minute."

Growling savagely, he hurled his weight against the rock. The second time I was with him . . . again and again . . . each time bringing further success . . . but that pursuing car was drawing nearer and nearer. Angrily I flung every ounce of my carcass against the damned boulder. . . .

"Look out!" Rug yelled warning. "She's going!"

And go she sure did! We ducked swiftly back, then scrambled down the hillside with that big rock bouncing ahead of us, leading the procession of hundreds of smaller boulders!

Once we'd reached bottom, out of the path of that avalanche, we paused to inspect our work. It was perfect! And that landslide wasn't yet finished. Rocks of all sizes and weights were still bouncing and careening down that slope, carrying small trees along with them. We kept back to a place of safety and watched. For a minute or so the noise was deafening and, despite the moonlight, we couldn't see a thing through the dense clouds of dust that rolled up before our eyes.

Then the dust settled and we saw that the road was filled from side to side with boulders, broken branches, small rocks, and dirt. The pass was so effectively blocked that no car would be able to get through until many hours had been spent clearing the way. There'd be no more pursuit from the rear. That much was absolutely certain.

Just then Santiago's voice reached us from down the road: "Ready, amigos! Move pronto!"

The moon chose that moment to again pass under a cloud, but the reflection of headlights behind the barrier we'd created partly lighted up the scene. I knew Rug and I were standing out as fine targets if anyone climbed to the top of that heap of boulders.

And someone did. I caught a glimpse of three heads as I started for the Hispano-

Avispa. There came a sudden command: "Halt or I fire!" Then a whole cyclone of curses in Spanish.

Rug and I paused to unleash some lead from our hawg legs. There was no time to pick marks; we were simply firing to spoil their aim until we could reach Santiago and Lamp.

A yelp of pain answered our efforts — then a ragged volley of rifle fire. Bullets were kicking up dust all around and whining past our ears as we sprinted toward the Hispano-Avispa which was already moving as we leaped to the running boards.

From behind came a torrent of baffled yells as Rug and I got back in our seats, our heads being nearly jerked off our shoulders as Santiago sent the big car leaping into high speed.

"Wait," I heard Rug exclaim. "I didn't figure to ride no more on this hurricane. Let me out. I'll take my chances with those ____"

That was all I heard. I reckon the swift rush of wind had cut off his breath. Me, I wasn't sure if I wanted any more riding either — not with Santiago doing the driving. He had the headlights off again as we ripped through the darkness. Lead was whining nastily all around us, but no one was hit. Call it luck or what you will. I don't pretend to explain it. Looking back, I could see crimson flashes of gunfire stabbing the gloom, but within a few moments we were too far away for the shots to be effective. I settled my Stetson on my head and got a firm grip on the side of the car. We were going so fast now I didn't dare jump out.

6. "WE'LL BE SHOT AS REBELS!"

We flashed on and on through the night. Once Santiago switched on his headlights, and I saw a big chuckhole in the road. Deftly he hurled the car around it and back to the center of the roadway — if that winding, twisting, rutty stretch of trail can be called a roadway. Anyway, I breathed a mite easier.

"Thought that chuckhole was along here someplace." The old war eagle chuckled. "I remembered it from this morning when I came down." Again he switched off the lights, then continued the conversation, congratulating Rug and me on the way we'd barred the road. Lamp had kept Santiago informed as to what we were doing while the damaged tire was removed and a good one slipped on the rim.

"Another hour should bring us to the border," Santiago commented, "providing nothing happens."

I'd noticed the road was growing a bit smoother now, so I knew we were drawing near the Federal outpost Santiago had mentioned. A couple of times when he'd switched on the lights I could see that the road was well traveled along here and, aside from a scattering of deep-rutted spots, was in pretty good condition.

Suddenly as we slowed to round a sharp curve I could see lights shining from buildings a mile or so farther on. Not just a few lights; the places were fairly blazing with illumination. As we drew nearer I could make out the figures of soldiers up ahead, their forms silhouetted against the yellow squares that lighted up the roadway.

The view wasn't reassuring by a long shot, but we were in for it now, and there was nothing to do but go through with the deal. I'm telling you, the cedar butt of my Colt gun was feeling plumb comforting in my hand about that time. Back in the tonneau I could hear Rug and Lamp getting ready for action.

Santiago had planned to leave his lights off and ride right on through. In that way we would have made a much more difficult mark for the carbines of the Federals. However, at the last moment he changed his mind — probably warned by some inner sense — and threw on his brights. Lucky for us he did! My heart had been jiggling around up in my throat someplace; now it seemed to suddenly stop dead. This time it sure looked like we were up against it for fair. There didn't seem to be any way out!

The instant Santiago switched on those lights I caught a picture that should have spelt finish in any man's language. There we were, hurtling through the night at a speed somewhere between sixty and eighty, with a deep ditch flanking either side of the roadway. And on either side, beyond the ditch, was a tightly strung barb-wire fence! Ahead our trail passed through a small town of scattered adobe huts, with to the right of the roadway a long, low building of the same construction — probably the Federal barracks.

Stretched directly across our path the soldiers had stacked a pile of heavy timbers! I've wondered since where so much wood came from all at once in that country, but there it was. Ten to one it had been freighted in to construct another barracks or something of the sort. Directly behind the timbers, standing breast high, was a line of

Mexican soldiers, their carbines ready for business. At one side of the road stood an officer, the raised sword in his hand emphasizing his command to halt. Other soldiers and civilians were scattered about, waiting for us to come to a stop. Right then there didn't seem to be anything else for us to do.

I glanced at Santiago, expecting him to throw on the brakes, but he drove on, straight ahead. Every second I was expecting him to pile us up on that heap of timbers. Scared? Say, I was paralyzed!

"*¿Quién vive?*" came the snarling challenge, high-pitched and questioning. Then, it seemed, everybody started yelling at once.

Summed up, those yells were meant for us to stop plenty pronto, but it was too late for that now. Santiago wasn't even slowing speed! My gun was in my hand, but I couldn't see when I'd get an opportunity to use it. Nearer and nearer we drove straight at that timbered barrier. I could almost see the whites of the soldiers' eyes now . . . could hear them cursing in obscene Spanish . . . saw them raise their carbines to shoulders. . . .

I half closed my eyes, bracing myself for the crash. Then I heard the brakes scream, and I was flung violently against the windshield. The car swerved crazily. God! Santiago had jammed on the brakes, released them, turned out at the last second — he'd left the trail and *leaped the ditch on his side of the road!* We were still going! *Still going!*

I saw the wheel jerk out of his hands as the car landed, sped on, straight through the barb-wire fence that bordered the far side of the ditch. Somewhere back of us came the snarling song of stretched, broken wire, filling the air with humming vibrations. Then Santiago got his grip again and jerked the big Hispano-Avispa savagely around just in time to avoid one of the adobe huts that loomed suddenly before us.

We were straightened out now, running parallel to the wire fence that stretched between us and the soldiers on the road. We'd lost valuable time though. I heard the order to fire, and a volley of rifle bullets thudded into the body of our car. Glass from the windshields splintered all around us. Some of the soldiers had retained sufficient presence of mind to catch Santiago's move even as he turned out to avoid the blocked roadway. Now they came leaping over the fence to cut us off.

I heard the roaring forty-fives in the seat behind me and knew that Rug and Lamp were holding up their end. Then I realized for the first time that my own six-shooter was jerking in my hand. One big fellow with open mouth and staring eyes leaped on the running board at my side. Even before I knew it my gun was spitting flame and smoke. The man's face abruptly fell away. Our right fender caught another soldier, threw him halfway across the road.

"Nice work," I caught from Santiago as he bent to his job; then a moment later, "Get this hombre on my side — quick!"

One of the soldiers had had sense enough to go for the driver, but even as I swung around to throw down on him I saw the barrel of Rug's forty-five crash against the fellow's head, and he, too, fell back into darkness.

We weren't free though by a long shot. The way was full of obstacles — rocks, ruts, and God knows what else. Some of the adobe huts were built mighty close to the fence, too, and we'd slowed down a lot. The soldiers were still coming behind us — also their bullets. Twice I clubbed men off the running board.

"We've got to chance it," I heard Santiago mutter, half to himself. The next instant he had steered the car back toward the roadway. I heard the taut strands of barbed wire snap like whipcord as we went back through the fence again. One fence post ripped off a

66

fender before it went down under our rush. Getting back across the ditch wasn't so easy this time though. We'd lost momentum. The front wheels struck just at the edge of the road, lost headway a moment. I thought we'd slip back and be caught like rats in a trap. The rear wheels were spinning madly, fighting to get traction. Soldiers were drawing near again, yelling and cursing like madmen. Their guns weren't idle, either. . . .

Then Santiago jammed his foot clear down on the accelerator. The next instant we had left the ditch. Say, once on level road that car leaped ahead like a shot out of a gun barrel. Santiago nearly turned us over, he was forced to straighten out so quick.

And then we were away once more. Only a few bullets were chasing us now, and I was commencing to breath easier when it happened.

I heard Santiago say something about it being a close call, then Lamp's grumbling tones, "Yeah, too damn' close — thank Gawd for the fun!" About that time something struck me a tremendous whack on top of the head, and red-hot steel seared my scalp. That's the way it felt, anyhow. . . .

When I came to I found myself back in the tonneau with Rug Wilton and Lamp. They'd dug up a flashlight someplace in the car and had it directed stright into my eyes. It was blinding and damn' irritating. I told them about it. My head felt kind of hot and sticky too. And ache? Say, ache's no word for what was happening to my top piece! "Dammit!" I crabbed. "Take that light out of my eyes."

I caught Rug's relieved sigh, "He's all right, Lamp. Any hombre that can swear like Stephens does isn't dead yet." The flashlight was switched off, then came Lamp's voice, "You dang-fool rannie, why didn't you tell us you were hit?"

"How in hell could I do that?" I answered with some irritation. "My lights went out the instant it happened."

"Naw," Lamp replied disgustedly, "I mean these slugs in your shoulder and that one on your left arm. Your knuckles are creased too. You must have got those wounds before this lead that parted your hair come along. Lucky for you it wasn't a sixteenth of an inch lower."

My brain was clearing a mite now. I said, "Oh yeah, those others. Shucks! They weren't bothering me to any extent, and I didn't want to boast for fear you two would be jealous."

I wasn't feeling so chipper at that. It was mighty comforting now just to take things easy and lean back against that rear cushion. My shirt was kind of warm and wet inside too. The jolting of the car made things sort of tough, but we were running free and easy by this time.

Santiago's voice drifted back to me now and then, but I don't remember whether he got an answer or not. Things had commenced to get blurry again, and my head was spinning like a drunken top.

Next time I woke up we had left the road and were cutting across the range. A few minutes later I saw the headlights flash on one of those white monuments that mark the international line between United States and Mexico, so I knew we were due to cross to safety within a few moments. The last thing I remember thinking was that we were mighty lucky we hadn't run into a border patrol of Federals along the way.

It must have been the stopping of the car that awakened me next time. I opened my eyes and stared around. We'd stopped up close to the door of a big adobe ranch house, and there were a lot of men gathered near. Then Santiago's voice, deep and courteous, "Come into your house, señores."

I knew then we'd arrived at some place belonging to Santiago. That's the way with the Spanish; when you visit 'em, they always speak of their property as yours. Kind of a nice custom at that. The next thing I knew was that Lamp and Rug were carrying me up some steps. I remember being mad at the time and telling them I could walk. Then things went black some more. A little later I gained consciousness long enough to find myself between fresh, clean blankets in a bed. I was feeling sort of weak and all in. Then I went under again.

7. Pascal Santiago's Story

I'd been sieved a heap worse than was at first thought. Nothing downright serious, you understand, but I was mighty weak from loss of blood. Luckily no bones had been broken; my hurts were all flesh wounds. Santiago got a doctor to the house the same night we arrived, and the doc dug such lead out of my carcass as hadn't gone on through.

At that, it was a full week before I stepped out of bed and another eight or nine days before I could get around without using a cane to walk with. I'm telling you, I'd lost a lot of my tan. I reckon I was a pretty pale, washed-out-looking hombre when I made my first appearance down at the bunkhouse where Rug and Lamp were living with the rest of Pascal Santiago's hands. I couldn't blame those two for laughing at me.

Lamp grinned when he saw me leaning heavy on my cane. "There's just three kinds of men carries canes," he chuckled. "Lame men, sick men, and damned fools."

"Meaning?" I asked.

"Meaning," Rug put in with a laugh, "that you're almost a mighty sick man now because you was damn' fool enough to help Santiago out of his scrape. No, not you alone. I think we were all damn' fools every time that ride we took comes to mind. Never again! I don't mind speeding so much, but I do crave to slow down on the curves — which same that old war eagle doesn't savvy how to do."

They walked out with me later to take a look at the Hispano-Avispa. Lord only knows how any of us escaped. The body was riddled with bullet holes; the windshield was gone; one fender was missing. The front bumper was bent back to a V shape. No, I didn't want another ride like that.

It was a nice outfit Santiago had. He ran the P-Bar-S iron, all prime-beef stuff, and made a pretty pile of jack doing it, too, even if he did spend most of his time at one or another of his other places. An owner can do that, though, when he has a good bunch of hands working for him and a reliable foreman like Tom Keene doing the rodding. It was a dang nice crew, and if any of them had ever heard of the Gila Shadow, it didn't seem to make any difference one way or the other to them.

There were a couple of breed women there, too, to do the cooking and housekeeping for the ranch and bunkhouse. That night, after supper at the ranch house, Santiago passed a box of cigars to Rug, Lamp, and me and opened the conversation:

"Now that Stephens is better and able to learn what it's all about, I think it's time I told the story."

Understand, we'd been in the dark all this time we'd been at the P-Bar-S. All we knew was that we'd helped extract Santiago from the jaws of death, as the saying goes. He hadn't offered to talk before this, and as none of us three wanted to exhibit our curiosity we hadn't asked any questions. Eager to hear what the deal was? I'll tell the world we were!

Santiago talked in English, and if I hadn't known he was Spanish I'd have sworn he was born north of the Rio Grande. He explained all that when he commenced.

"I was educated at the University of Madrid, took a thorough course in English over there, so you see I had a good basis in your language to begin with. My people were what is considered wealthy in Spain, so when I had completed my schooling and evinced a desire to travel to South America they furnished me a very tidy sum of money to start on."

He paused a moment to touch a lighted match to his cigar, then went on, "I won't go into the minor details of my early struggles to learn all there was to learn about the raising and selling of beef. Eventually I bought cattle of my own. My herds increased rapidly, and when I sold out my holdings I received a very large sum of money. In short, I had become what is known in this country as a millionaire. I was still a young man, remember, so when stories of Mexico reached my ears I got the wanderlust. Instead of returning to Spain as I had intended, I journeyed to Mexico City. There I met my fate in the person of Señorita Isabel Alvarado, whose family was among those most prominent in the social circles of the capital city."

Santiago paused as his lips tightened a bit grimly, then continued, "At the time I left the Argentine in South America to come to

Mexico I was accompanied by another man. His real name doesn't matter, but he is known as El Gato Montés."

"Mountain cat, eh?" Rug translated.

Santiago nodded. "That's near enough. Some call him a tiger. The name is appropriate in many ways, with the one exception that he lacks the cat's, or the tiger's, cunning. He is a brutish, savage creature, with small regard for man or beast. He'd killed a man in the Argentine during a drunken brawl, and when he begged me to take him with me I took pity on him and paid his way to Mexico City. Otherwise he'd have had to pay for his crime in Argentina. It was a foolish move on my part; I've regretted it more than once, but at that time I felt there might be a chance of the man's turning honest. I should have known better. He has a bad combination of mixed bloods coursing his veins — and no animal is ever better than its breeding."

Santiago flicked the ash from his cigar and resumed, "The money I'd given El Gato Montés when we reached Mexico City didn't last long — too many women and too much liquor. I gained his enmity when I refused to give him further financial aid. He had little education and less polish, so he pulled certain wires and gained a commission as lieutenant in the Mexican army, using that position as a leverage to boost himself into society. It was then that he met Señorita Isabel Alvarado. El Gato did his best to persuade her to marry him, but her people favored me — as she did — and it was I who won her hand. El Gato's enmity for me increased accordingly, of course."

There was a wistful smile on Santiago's face as he continued: "My wife gave me two children, a boy and a girl. At present the boy, Ramon, is about your age, Stephens — if he still lives —— Wait" — holding up one hand — "you'll see what I mean when I've talked further. Paula, my daughter, is seven years younger and is attending a university in California. I've kept her in the States for the past ten years. Mexico has been somewhat unsettled, you see. . . . But to get back to my story — Doña Isabel and I had retired to make our home in Chihuahua City with our children, but three years after Paula was born my wife died. To forget my grief I plunged deeply into business. The affairs of Mexico were in a bad state, so I invested most of my money in the United States but continued to live in Chihuahua. My children were growing up, and I wanted them taken care of, you understand."

I reckon Santiago thought we were getting

restless, because everything he'd said so far didn't seen to have any bearing on what had happened at the Golden Cactus that night. Anyway, there was a note of apology in his tones as he went on: "I appear to be going away back in my telling of this story, but it's all necessary if you're to understand just where El Gato Montés fits into my life. During the Argentine days he and I were little more than mere acquaintances; since then he has been responsible for most of the misfortune that has come to me. However, as the years passed in Mexico he grew in power with the different administrations, dropping back to the army from time to time when some fresh influence would get to work on the President of Mexico or when a revolution occurred. The last I heard of him he was a captain of infantry, so his luck has probably changed for the worse again."

"Hombres like El Gato Montés," Rug cut in, "never do see to stay on top long. In the end somebody always catches up to 'em."

"As I hope to catch up to him someday," Santiago said savagely. His eyes glowed hotly for a moment, then he shrugged his powerful shoulders and continued, "Meanwhile I'd been growing stronger and stronger with the Mexican government, while El Gato was trying to get a foothold in state affairs. For a time I was retained in an advisory capacity in the Treasury Department. The Presidente was friendly and, almost before I knew it, I had been made president of the Banco de Dinero in Chihuahua."

Santiago laughed and said, "There was more honor than anything else in my appointment. The finances of Mexico were in bad shape at that period; the Banco de Dinero was on the verge of failure. However, as I said, the Presidente was friendly and I was anxious to help all I could. To be brief, I agreed to place two hundred fifty thousand pesos of my own money at the bank's disposal, providing the Mexican government would do the same. The Presidente answered my proposal by sending me the money. The Banco de Dinero had, therefore, five hundred thousand pesos with which to regain its financial stability."

"Jeepers!" Lamp gasped. "That's nigh a quarter of a million in American money!"

"Just about." Santiago nodded. "At that time the Banco de Dinero was undergoing some repairs, so I swore the workmen to secrecy and had a special iron column installed in which I secreted the money. I figured it would be safer there until things had quieted down. At the time I thought the idea a good one; now I know differently. Evidently the workmen guessed what I was going to use that column for — one or more of them must have talked ——" He broke off suddenly, then asked, "You've all heard of Pablo Vinada, haven't you?"

We nodded. Who hasn't heard of Pablo Vinada, the once-great bandit leader? Once he almost succeeded in getting himself made Presidente of Mexico. He was famous — or infamous — for his raids along the United States border, if nothing else.

"You'll remember, then" — Santiago again took up his story — "that seven years ago Vinada and his *bandidos* succeeded in capturing and holding Mexico City for three days. He had intended getting himself elected to the chair of the Presidente, but he wasn't quite strong enough for that. He did loot the treasury, though, for something like three million. That money he brought by train up north as far as Jiménez. There he sidetracked the train sometime after midnight, packed the money on mules, and carried it away into the hills. There were only four men with him when he headed into the hills, and it is said that he shot and killed those four that he might keep the secret of the hiding place to himself."

Lamp said, "Didn't anybody ever find the

place the money was buried?"

"I'll get to that part shortly," Santiago replied. "Three months later Vinada and his army of rebels, or bandits — call them what you will — went on another raid. They swooped down on Chihuahua City. The town was practically surprised off its feet, so Vinada had no trouble holding it at bay while he robbed the Banco de Dinero. He located the iron column where I had secreted the five hundred thousand pesos and broke into it. Then, like the money he had stolen from the national treasury, he packed the silver away on mules to a secret hiding place. This time he took only two men with him — and as before shot them, so he could have the secret to himself."

"And your Banco de Dinero was busted again, eh?" Rug asked.

Santiago nodded. "If they had given me half a chance I would have been willing to make good the loss out of my own pocket, but here's where El Gato Montés saw an opportunity to discredit me with the Mexican government, and he did it, being in favor at that time with those high in the councils of the administration. El Gato claimed I had engineered the whole deal and that I knew, as well as Pablo Vinada, the secret hiding place of the stolen money.

Naturally I made denials, but it was no use. No one believed me in that first panic of excitement. Despite the fact I had been useful to the government a warrant was issued for my arrest. There was a death penalty attached, providing I was captured. I realized it would look bad if I ran away. On the other hand, if I remained nothing but death stared me in the face."

Santiago smiled. "And so I fled, escaped to California, before the soldiers arrived to arrest me. A friend had warned me of their coming. Luckily both my son and daughter were in the United States at the time. The Mexican administration has changed hands; there's another Presidente in the chair, but to this day the warrant for my death is in force. The instant I am apprehended in Mexico they'll stand me against a wall and call it a traitor's death when a firing squad sends its bullets into my body. So now" — and Santiago's eyes twinkled — "you boys will understand why I didn't stop to pick any daisies that night on the ride home from the Golden Cactus."

8. A Man-Sized Job

Rug chuckled. "Maybe you didn't stop to pick daisies, Mister Santiago, but for a spell there I sure thought somebody would be furnishing us with lilies."

"My haste" — Santiago smiled — "was more than necessary. I think you'll agree."

We agreed all right. There were more things we wanted to know. What had taken him to the Golden Cactus in the first place? I felt pretty sure we didn't have all the story. Another thing, being right in my line, you might say, I was a heap interested in the money Pablo Vinada had stolen and hidden away. I asked, "How about that money Vinada buried? Did he ever go back for it, or didn't he have time?"

Santiago shook his head. "News leaks out, one way or another. Mostly what we know was learned from certain of Vinada's followers who were captured after a time. Briefly here's what we know: after the money from the Banco de Dinero had been hidden Vinada returned to his band of rebels. Three days later his dead body was brought in. He had been shot from behind. That took place over seven years ago, and to this day they've never learned who killed him."

"Then nobody ever found the money he'd stolen from the treasury, eh?" Lamp asked.

Santiago's hands opened in a gesture of helplessness. "How could they? It was a secret hiding place, and Vinada had shot the men who had accompanied him, as he himself later boasted."

"How about your money and that of the government's that was taken from the iron column in the Banco de Dinero?" I asked.

"Ah, that's a different matter — perhaps," Santiago replied. "A number of expeditions, both American and Mexican, have searched for that money, but they've never found it. I had just about given up hope of every hearing of it again, when about five months ago I received some news that placed an entirely different face on the matter. My son Ramon some six months ago suddenly disappeared from our home. A month later I received a letter from him stating that he was on the trail of the missing Banco de Dinero money and not to worry. Naturally I did worry. He had given me an address where I could correspond with him, and, while it was a risky, foolish thing to do, we exchanged letters. In his next letter I learned he had joined an army of rebels. It had been necessary, he wrote, though he had no interest in the national politics of Mexico. I immediately wrote him to return at once to the United States before he got into trouble. This time there was no reply. Again I wrote, but again I received no answer to my letter."

"It doesn't sound so good," Rug muttered, half to himself.

"I feared something had happened to the boy," Santiago went on. "Growing desperate, I wrote a long letter to the government at Mexico City and placed the whole matter before the heads. However, the government is on a stronger basis now than it has ever been — at least to my way of thinking — and it was reluctant to bring up any old matter that might weaken its position. I wanted permission to go down into Mexico. There was a good deal of red tape about the whole affair, and the upshot of the matter was that the government wouldn't give its permission — officially. I'm afraid some of the heads there didn't believe my story. The best I could get were some papers giving me safe conduct, providing I could, at the time I showed the papers, also give information as to the hiding place of the money taken from the Banco de Dinero. . . . Now I'd like to find that money and turn back the half the government had advanced from its treasury. I want to prove I'm no thief. It's a matter of pride; don't you see?" Santiago's voice faltered a trifle as he added, "I want mostly to find my son and bring him back in safety. But I don't dare go searching for him."

Rug commented sympathetically, "It looks to me like you were up against a stone wall. Still, in a way, I can't blame the Mex government for the stand it took. It's only natural it would want its own game to run smooth. For all they know, maybe you were mixed up with rebels. The government has to look out for its own welfare first."

"That is very true," Santiago agreed instantly.

"I'm still wondering," Lamp put in, "what brought you to the Golden Cactus."

"I'm getting to that part of the story now." Santiago nodded. "What brought me to Chili Joe's place was a note I received. The note was unsigned, but it stated that for the sum of five thousand dollars I could have news regarding the whereabouts of my son if I'd come to the Golden Cactus that night. I thought of it being a trap but decided to take a chance. Luckily one of Joe's waiters is an old servant of mine, and he overheard the assassins making plans for my murder. I was warned in time and, thanks to you three boys, I escaped unharmed."

I asked, "Who do you suppose was responsible for that note?"

"I don't know for certain," Santiago said, "but I feel almost sure it was El Gato Montés. Of course I have no proof. It's just

84

a hunch, as you *Americanos* say. It may be that El Gato has information regarding the fact that Ramon is on the track of the missing Banco de Dinero money and wants the pesos for himself. On the other hand, he hates me and would go to any length to bring about my death. One thing is certain, the assassin, whoever he is, didn't have soldiers with him, so I feel sure the Mexican government wasn't back of the plot. The men who attacked us at the Golden Cactus were just plain border scum. Of course when we escaped from the Golden Cactus somebody warned the army post that we were coming. Likely they said we were escaped rebels. I took a long chance going below the border in the first place. And it wouldn't be healthy for any of us to be recognized back there again. Yes, I'm practically certain El Gato Montés was back of the move to kill me."

Lamp said dryly, "I'm commencing to understand why you and El Gato don't cater to each other too much."

Santiago's eyes burned with a hard brittle light for a moment, and when I looked into them I was sure glad he wasn't my enemy. He spoke in slow measured tones: "Someday El Gato Montés and I are going to meet again. When we do, may the *buen Dios* pity him. You see, I learned but recently from a former follower of his that my wife didn't die a natural death. El Gato Montés hired a servant to poison her. Oh yes, I'm fully prepared for El Gato when we meet face to face."

Maybe you think that information didn't make us sit straighter in our chairs. It made us realize just what sort of brute this El Gato Montés was. However, it was quite a spell later before I learned just what Santiago meant when he said he was "fully prepared."

None of us spoke for a time. Santiago called to one of the breed women to bring another pot of coffee and a bottle of bourbon. We lighted fresh cigars. Blue smoke drifted lazily through the ranch-house dining room to be wafted up the chimney of a fireplace in one corner where a small fire of mesquite roots took the chill from the cool night air. Once or twice I noticed Santiago turn his glance my way as though about to speak. Somehow I had an impression he had a proposition of some sort to place before me.

At last I broke the silence: "Well, what's the next move? If I can help, just say the word."

The sudden look Santiago flashed in my

direction was warming. Right away I wanted more than ever to help him out of his trouble, but I didn't know just where to commence, or how.

"Before I answer your question," Santiago replied quietly, "I want to ask one of my own. Just why are you called the Gila Shadow?"

I sort of caught my breath for a minute. I didn't know what he was driving at. Lamp and Rug were watching me with sudden interest too. Not that I cared so much; they were my friends and I knew it. But bringing up that Gila Shadow name and all it stood for made me feel mighty uncomfortable for a spell.

I could feel my face growing hot. "Why — er — I don't know exactly," I stammered. I wasn't as proud of that name as I had been a few weeks before. Then the name had stood for a stick-up man who had the whole Southwest country standing on its ear. Probably it still stood for the same thing, but all of a sudden I realized what a cheap hombre I must appear to white men. I finally found my tongue: "Gila is a nickname I've had ever since I was a kid. It was tacked onto me because I had one of those Gila lizards — Gila monsters, folks call 'em — for a pet in those days. People could never understand why it didn't bite me, but shucks, those lizards get plumb tame with decent handling. . . ." I paused suddenly. This was getting off the track. I knew I might as well come clean with Santiago. My eyes met his squarely. "The Shadow part of the name — well, some dang sheriff fastened that on me. He said chasing me was like trying to catch a shadow."

"Meaning you were plumb slippery in making a getaway, eh?" Rug commented.

My career was nothing to be proud of, but just the same I caught a gleam of admiration in Rug's glance. I commenced to feel better, even if I was ashamed of my life by now — rather what it stood for. I tried to laugh it off. "Mostly the sheriffs that chased me had bad breaks in their luck. I was always a lucky hombre."

Santiago nodded. "I guess we all know how lucky you were and what 'bad breaks' those sheriffs received. The fact remains, Dale Stephens, that you have brains. It requires brains to elude the law as long as you have. I've checked up considerably on your life the past days you've been convalescing here, and from everywhere — even from your worst enemies — comes word that you have a habit of giving the other fellow all the best of the deal."

"Aw-w-w!" I protested, and my ears were burning like the devil. I couldn't find the words to say more right at the moment.

All three were laughing at me now, and there I was, sitting there with no way to defend myself. Santiago asked next, "What started you in this holdup game, anyway?"

I told them the whole story as quickly as possible. How I was learning to punch cows when I was just a button and how one night when I rode to town my boss was held up and robbed. I didn't even know he was away from the ranch that night, but somehow I got blamed for it when folks heard I'd gone to town to order a new saddle. It didn't do any good to tell 'em I'd saved up my wages to get that saddle. Hell! Cow pokes don't know how to save money, generally, and nobody will believe a kid when he's in a tight. At least those folks didn't believe me. Later on the real robber was caught, but by that time I'd had a bad name tacked to me and it stuck. I didn't have a father or mother to stand up for me. I'd just got off to a bad start, that's all, through no fault of my own.

"How old were you at that time?" Santiago asked.

"A mite past fifteen years."

"¡*Valgame Dios!*" Santiago gasped. "A mere

child! And do you like it, this holdup business?"

Right then and there I unburdened my mind of a heap of things that had been piling up for years. I told him in no uncertain terms just what I thought of holdup men, including myself. I don't know, maybe my feelings sort of carried me away, but I sure made myself plain. ". . . so you see," I concluded, "aside from the thrills and the fun of taking risks, there's nothing to it. I'd sooner punch cows. But what was I to do? Nobody would give me a job. I had to live. So you see, in a way I was forced into the holdup game. If I'd been older I'd have known better, but I was feeling pretty bitter those days, and I wanted to hurt everybody the way I'd been hurt. Once in a while I'd reform, take a different name and find a job, but before long the truth always came out, and I'd be forced to do some pronto sloping and return to holding up banks and robbing stages. Just before I turned that Cashton Savings Bank trick I'd held a job for over a year. Then a snoopy range dick turned up, and I had to high-tail it in another direction."

"By the way," Santiago interposed softly, "what became of the money you got from the Cashton Bank? That night I met you,

you were flat broke."

"I've got it cached in a safe place," I answered. "In a bank in El Paso del Norte — safest place in the world to keep money when you're traveling fast and don't want to be caught with stolen money on you."

Santiago nodded slowly. "Providing some other Gila Shadow doesn't hold up the El Paso bank."

"There isn't any other Gila Shadow." I grinned. "Anyway, the bank would make good."

"Quite so," Santiago said quietly. "And does it pay well, this business you follow?"

"Pay hell!" I said disgustedly. "What you get you never get a chance to spend among decent folks — yet it's gone before you realize it, and there's one more charge chalked against your name. Nope, it's one *muy malo* game to play. You never win in the long run — nor, I reckon, in the short run, either."

Again Santiago nodded. "I know something of that too, amigo. I've heard a great deal about the things you've done with your money. I told you I'd been checking up on you. I've had a detective agency working on your trail, if you care to know it." He cut short my exclamation of surprise and went on, "Yes, I've learned quite a few things regarding your use of stolen money. As I understand it, poor people receive most of your funds. I heard of a widow with three children who needed cash to save her ranch. There was another case of a tuberculosis hospital receiving a nice donation. Then there was that mine-relief fund. Wasn't there a sick rancher over near Tucson who needed money for an operation? And, let's see, there was that cowboy who broke his back busting broncs. Gila Shadow, you lied to us; you haven't a red cent in that El Paso bank!"

I just stared. I know my mouth was hanging wide open. Cripes! I was too surprised to speak while he reeled off a long list of things that I'd done — er — that he'd heard I'd done. I don't know where he ever got such crazy ideas. I felt myself getting madder and madder. There was no sense bringing up that stuff anyway.

"Aw-w-w!" I sputtered, and I know my face was the color of ripe beets. "Somebody's been running a whizzer on you. You mustn't believe everything you hear. Just because I gave away a couple of bucks to a charity bazaar one time is no sign I'm one of these here philanthropists."

"Whew!" Lamp Lamonte whistled. "There's a ten-dollar word if I ever heard one. Where'd you hear it?"

"I read it" — I laughed — "in a library in

Phoenix. I've spent a heap of time in libraries around the Southwest while sheriffs were scouring the country looking for me."

"My Gawd!" Rug burst out. "No wonder they never caught you. I suppose you'll be telling us next that you've read some of this Bill Shakespeare's books."

"Some," I admitted. "I was always sort of partial to this Mark Twain hombre though. He writes a lot of funny stuff, but there's more to him than that if you read between the lines."

Lamp said gravely, "You've probably endowed a heap of libraries with that money you've picked up from time to time."

Mister, I was taking a ribbing, no doubt of that. I tried to change the subject: "Jeepers! I never got all the money folks said I did, anyway. I was blamed for a lot of jobs I never pulled. Every time there was a holdup and the sheriff was too busy or too lazy to go after his man he'd blame it on me. Folks never expected the Gila Shadow to be caught." Try as I would, I couldn't keep a touch of pride out of my tones as I said that.

"All right, we'll take your word for it." Santiago chuckled.

Rug and Lamp were snickering to themselves. I glared at 'em, and right away they sobered up. I turned to Santiago. "What's the idea in all the questions, anyway?"

Santiago said quietly, "I just wanted to know the sort of man who was going back into Mexico to locate my son Ramon for me, Dale."

His words almost swept me out of my chair. I hadn't been prepared for anything of that kind. I gulped a couple of times, but I couldn't find my voice to reply.

"That is," Santiago continued, "if you'll take the job." His voice sounded far away in my ears. I couldn't realize he was speaking to me. "You see, I can't go down there myself — at least I don't want to chance it until there's something more definite to go on. You know the country and the language. You've plenty of nerve — not to mention brains. You'll pardon me for saying so, I hope, but if anyone should recognize you, he won't think it strange that the Gila Shadow is taking a vacation — shall we say? — from his own country. Such things are understood in Mexico. Of course there's a certain amount of risk involved, but I'm going to make things as easy as possible. I'll pull some wires and get a special permit for you to carry. You'll simply pretend to be on a hunting trip. A good deal of tan has bleached out of your face, so you won't look as though you were accustomed to a life in the open. How about it?"

I was still staring at him, wide-eyed. I did manage to stammer, "How in the name of the seven bald steers am I going to find your son when I don't even know what he looks like, or where he is?"

"I know it's a difficult proposition" — Santiago frowned — "but if you take the job you'll just have to trust to luck. I've a picture of Ramon here; that may help some."

He rose from the table and left the room. In a minute he returned with four photographs which he handed to me. I looked at the first one. Young Ramon resembled his dad a heap, I could see at the first glance. The next two pictures had been taken when he was younger, but I knew already that if I ever set eyes on him I wouldn't make any mistake about his identity.

The fourth photograph brought a surprise. Instead of Ramon it was a picture of a girl, Ramon's sister Paula. I knew that the instant I looked at it.

"My daughter," Santiago was saying. "If it wasn't for her I'd chance going in search of Ramon myself."

Right then I felt my eyes getting sort of misty. Santiago was getting into me more every minute. When a man like Pascal

Santiago shows a picture of his daughter to an outlaw like the Gila Shadow, it proves — well, there's a mighty firm friendship there; that's all. I looked at Paula's picture again. She was Santiago all over, except her lines were soft where his were firm. I don't mean there was anything weak about her looks. There was plenty determination in her eyes and chin and mouth; her face was oval-shaped with arched eyebrows and soft dark hair about her temples. Pretty? Not exactly. Something more than pretty. Lots of character in her face too. I was seeing, right that minute, for the first time what the word "woman" means. Nothing of your clinging-vine type there. Paula looked to be the sort of girl with a world of nerve who could take care of herself in any situation.

Gosh! I sure hated to give up that picture when Santiago passed the photographs across to Rug and Lamp. I knew right then I was going to take that job Santiago offered, but I wasn't doing it just for him, or for Ramon either; I was doing it for Paula. I was still in a sort of daze. I reckon Santiago figured I was scary about taking a chance returning to Mexico.

"Of course all of your expenses will be paid," he was saying, looking hopefully at me. "As to salary — well, if you locate Ramon and find the money Vinada stole from the Banco de Dinero, half of it will be yours. All I ask is the Mexican government's share that I may return and prove that Pascal Santiago isn't a thief."

There was nothing halfway about the man. Things were coming too fast for me to grasp, and I could only nod dumbly. His grip when he took my hand meant more than could be put into words. Looking back at it now, he must have thought I was an inarticulate sort of hombre, or maybe just plain stupid. If he'd only known it, I'd have been pleased to go for nothing, let alone one hundred twenty-five thousand dollars.

It didn't occur to me then that finding a hombre I'd never seen, with all of Mexico to search in, was a real man-sized job. I only knew that I was happier than I'd ever been in my life, and that night when I rolled into bed I couldn't get to sleep for seeing a pair of friendly dark eyes looking at me. Maybe I was only dreaming, but they were Paula's eyes sure enough.

9. "I'm After Big Game"

If it had been left to me I'd have started off early the next morning, but Santiago just laughed at my eagerness. He figured I wasn't strong enough yet to stand the gaff of a long trail in the saddle, so he insisted on my waiting a while longer.

Finally I did get to do some riding so as to limber up my saddle muscles and get the feel of leather between my legs again. There were half a dozen saddles, almost new, at the P-Bar-S, and I had my pick of the bunch. I chose a nice center-fire rig, and out in the saddlers' corral I found the horse to fit it — a nice straight-legged roan gelding with good eyes and a nice width in the chest. His coat was sleek and he looked like a space eater to me. From the first that horse and me took to each other like brothers.

Santiago was away from the ranch for several days, and when he returned he brought a nice new Winchester thirty-thirty repeating rifle and an extra six-shooter for me. I'm telling you, he wasn't overlooking anything. He'd used his pull in various directions, too, and got somebody on the American side of the border to procure some papers for me to take along. Not that we were expecting much help from the special permit, only the old war eagle was placing his chips on everything that might help. As for me, I doubted considerable that anybody would believe I was on a hunting trip when I got down below the border.

Santiago suggested that I take a pack horse along, too, to carry grub, and so on, but I vetoed that idea. I figured I might be drifting fast someplace and I didn't want to be held up waiting for any pack horse. I was aiming to travel light, you understand.

Before I started Rug Wilton and Lamp Lamonte had taken a *pasear* down to Tia Lucia to get the horses they'd left at the livery there the night I met them. Mostly they wanted to learn if our rumpus at the Golden Cactus and what followed had caused any comment around the town, but when they came back two days later they didn't have a thing to report, except that everything seemed quiet. That proved something, anyway: the attack on Santiago hadn't been instigated by the Mexican government. It certainly looked like El Gato Montés had had his finger in the pie — on second thought, he'd probably cooked up the damn' dish himself.

Eventually I got started. Rug and Lamp wanted to accompany me, but we all agreed it was a one-man job — at least until I could learn something definite. Santiago already had them on his pay roll, though, and they were ready to come a-runnin' the instant I sent word. The two of them and Santiago accompanied me as far as the border. My departure was timed so I could slip over the line at night; there wasn't so much chance of being spotted after dark.

I can remember the morning we pulled away from the ranch just as plainly as though it were yesterday. Santiago was in regulation range togs, and although he must have been well past fifty he climbed into that saddle with all the liveliness of a youngster, sat that horse like a centaur, too, as though he'd been born on a bronc's back. Believe me, he didn't look or act his age by a long shot. He was wiry, tough, and as hard as nails.

I noticed toward the end of the journey to the border, though, that he grew sort of quiet, and while I didn't mention the fact I was doing a heap of thinking. Finally when we had reached the line it all came out. At the last minute, when it came time to say goodby, Santiago changed his mind. He'd been mulling over the whole setup and decided the risk was too great for me to take.

I just laughed when he mentioned his fears. I was really rarin' to go about that time, and after a lot of fast talking I finally persuaded him there wasn't going to be any danger. He didn't say anything more after that, but I felt he wasn't convinced — not entirely. The handclasps those three gave me when my time came to go on alone was something to swear by. They didn't say much; that wasn't necessary with them gripping my hand like it was something they hated to let go of. And, mister, I was feeling the same way.

"You goldarn box-ankled, gall-sored ol' son of a sheepherder," Lamp said, squeezing my fingers like I thought I'd never get to handle a six-gun again, "I hopes they pick you up first thing and stands you against a 'dobe wall."

"Either that," Rug adds, "or maybe you'll have some good luck and get stacked out on an anthill with honey smeared on your carcass. Try and keep us informed of what do they do to you, eh? We wouldn't want you to enjoy this vacation too much."

There wasn't much light, the moon being clouded over considerable, but I could see something sort of glistening in their eyes, and they gulped some over the words. Cripes! Those danged rannies talking that-away commenced to get on my nerves. It was all foolishness. I'd been on lots riskier trails before. Anyway, I considered their feelings and hastened to get started.

We all laughed some then, but it didn't

sound natural nohow. I don't know what's wrong with some hombres, but those three couldn't say good-by without fussing over it. Anyway, I finally yanked my hand loose to reach my bandanna. There was some dust got in my eyes. Then I jabbed spurs to my horse's ribs and we got started. I turned back in the saddle after my bronc had covered a short distance and could see the three of 'em still standing there in the gloom, then I caught Santiago's voice through the night air: "*Adiós,* my son. *Vaya con Dios.* Go with God."

I managed to call back an adiós, but I was kind of choked up. Santiago calling me his son in that way got to me strong. You see, it had been a mighty long time since anybody had called me "son." Santiago may have been Spanish, but he sure was white clear through — like the majority of Spanish I've met since those days. I've talked to a lot of hotheads who say they don't like Mexicans. In my opinion they're crazy — I mean the hotheads. There's good and bad in all races, and I've found when you give a Mexican a fair deal he'll do the same by you.

Those were my thoughts as I rode away, leaving my friends in the darkness. Things were sort of blurred for a spell, and by the time I got the dust cleared from my eyes my bronc was just carrying me past one of those white stones that mark the border line. I turned to look back once more, but it was too dark to see anything. I listened and could hear faintly the sounds made by running hoofs, but about that time a coyote off on a mesa starts in his yip-yip-yipping, and the sounds of the horses were lost in the echoes that went rolling off through the sandy hills.

I traveled all night, doing a heap of thinking and watching the moon float across the sky when it wasn't obscured by clouds. There was a soft breeze blowing, too, but as morning drew near it died away. Along toward dawn a sort of grayish-pink glow commenced to spread along the eastern horizon. I knew my bronc was getting a mite weary. He'd been traveling steady with never a letup and covered a heap of miles since I said good-by to Santiago and Rug and Lamp the previous night. Being it was the longest stretch I'd spent in the saddle in many a day, I was ready to crawl down and get some shut-eye.

It grew lighter. I was passing through hilly country. In fact, I was surrounded by hills until, like the feller says, I couldn't see the scenery. Just hills covered with mesquite and those big sahuaro cactuses and prickly pear. I knew there wouldn't be much chance of my being seen by this time by any of the law authorities that might be riding about. Not that it worried me much; I was a considerable distance from the border by now. The posse that had been trailing me for the Cashton job had given up and returned to the States some two weeks before. Pascal Santiago had learned that much for me, so I was feeling easier.

The sun was just pushing above the hills when I pulled to a halt and climbed down. I was some stiff, at that. The brush was growing high at this spot, and there was some vegetation my pony could nibble on. I ate a couple of biscuits and some bacon I carried, drank a few swallows from my canteen, then poured the remainder of the water into my Stetson for the bronc to suck up. After that I removed his saddle, staked him out, and spread my blankets.

It was around noon when I opened my eyes — too blamed hot to start traveling at once. For two-three hours I sat smoking cigarettes in the shade of a juniper bush. Not much shade, to be sure, but still it was better than being completely unprotected under that fierce white sun. Finally I threw my rig across the roan's back and we got started again.

Toward evening as I circled a hill I came on a flock of sheep. Dirty, smelly, greasy beasts they were, too, with their silly blatting. Me, I never could stand sheep. They were pretty well spread out, and I didn't at first see who was herding them, though I did hear a dog barking at the far side of the flock. Then up on a slope a short spell away I spied one of those blocky dobe shacks. It sort of blended with the colors of the hillside, and if it hadn't been for a white-washed door and four or five strings of red chili peppers hung from rafter ends to dry, I might have missed the place completely.

I headed my bronc up the hill, past the sheep, figuring to get some food and water at the house. Suddenly as I reached the far rim of the flock a Mex shepherd got up from where he'd been lounging on the ground. He was a mean-looking cuss, with beady black eyes and a round greasy face. He looked me over while I was taking in his print shirt and faded overalls. A pair of tattered sandals of rope and leather partly covered the dirtiest feet I've ever seen. There was a feather jutting from the hatband of his floppy sombrero; I guessed he was part Apache or Yaquente blood.

I pulled my roan to a stop. "*¿Cómo stá?*" I greeted him.

He didn't answer for a moment as he stood there chasing the animal life around inside his shirt and eying me with a heap of suspicion in his eyes. Finally his hand emerged from its hunting expedition, and he gave a short grunt to let me know the conversation could continue.

"Señor," I informed him in Spanish, "I want food and water."

"You have the peso?" he whined.

I reached into my pocket, pulled out a silver dollar, and tossed it to him. He caught it with a movement that was faster than I figured he was capable of making, and his little pig eyes lighted up with a greedy sparkle. He bit down on the dollar a couple of times to see if it was genuine, then, "It is not enough, señor. I must have another."

I wasn't wasting any time along that line. "Return it," I said shortly. "Doubtless I can find, farther on, food less expensive."

With that he gave a sly grin, pocketed the dollar, and turned up the slope toward the house. I knew I'd won, so I kicked my pony in the side and followed him up the hill.

One thing that caught my eye as I dismounted in front of the house was a modern repeating rifle standing near the door. Right then I had a hunch my host was mixed up in other dirty business aside from his sheep.

Howsomever, I didn't say anything, although I half expected to find a crew of rebels waiting for me just inside the door.

I was wrong though. There was nobody inside except a wrinkle-faced Yaqui woman in a loose-fitting dress padding around barefooted on the earthern floor. At one end of the room was a small fireplace with a kettle of some sort of stew bubbling away and making steam. Two chairs and a table stood in the center of the room, and in one corner was a rumpled heap of filthy blankets.

My sheepherder host made talk in the woman's own language, telling her what I wanted. She nodded and lazily rid herself of a couple of grunts. Then he turned back to me: "And your name, señor?" he inquired.

"You'll find it in the social register," I told him. Somehow he didn't appreciate my humor; he just blinked. I said, "Oh hell, I'll save you the trouble of looking me up. The name's Stephens, if you have to know."

"I," he continued loftily, "am Pedro Devaca. Be seated, and while you await the food I would tell you of my family. I am of the blood of the purest Castilian ——"

"That's to be seen at a glance" — I cut him short, not appreciating his humor either — "but I'm hungry, Señor Devaca." I knew he was a liar, of course, so far as that Castilian-blood idea went. I never knew it to fail: the more mixed bloods they have in their veins, the more they shout about their noble lineage. Anyway, I had no desire to indulge in a long-winded conversation. I'd noticed the woman hadn't yet made any attempt to get my food on the table, and I had a hunch Devaca was trying to hold up the proceedings until some of his friends arrived. "I'm hungry," I added, "and I must be on my way, señor. I can wait no longer."

My words didn't set well with Devaca. His pig eyes got tiny red pin points in 'em, but I stared right back, and finally he turned to the woman and ordered her to get food on the table. Even then she didn't show much speed, so I brought up the matter of water for my horse.

That brought on more whining and a lot of talk about water being scarce, but another dollar got action. Devaca shuffled outside and returned with a pail of water. I filled the canteen on my saddle and gave the rest to my pony.

By the time I stepped back into the house a steaming bowl of stew and a plate of cold tortillas were on the table. That stew was a mess, all right — goat's liver, onions, garlic, mutton, frijoles, chili peppers, Lord only knows what else — but it wasn't so bad for a hungry man, even if I did wonder once or twice if the strange flavor was the result of rattlesnake meat or coyote flesh. Maybe I shouldn't criticize that stew; I had a second helping. Devaca didn't join me in the meal, so I judged he was waiting for someone else to put in an appearance, particularly in view of the fact he'd gone to the doorway a couple of times and looked around the horizon.

I had the right hunch all right: about the time I was nearly through with my food I heard a horse stop in front of the house. A few minutes later a man stuck his head through the doorway, then stepped inside. Right away I guessed him to be some renegade puncher from the States. He was a hard-looking hombre in a dirty shirt and worn overalls. There was a six-shooter strapped at his right hip. There was no chance of his using it though — at least not for quick work. Part of his shirt had been cut away, and his right shoulder was swathed in filthy-looking bandages. He looked sort of pale and drawn, so I judged he hadn't been stirring around for many days.

The instant he spoke to Devaca I caught a familiar tone in his voice. Then it came to me where I'd seen him. He was the feller who had been standing on the running board of the machine-gun car in front of the Golden Cactus the night the attempt was made on Pascal Santiago's life! Now I understood the bandaged shoulder; it was one of my bullets had been responsible for that.

He looked me over with a lot of suspicion showing in his eyes while Devaca took care of the introduction. His damaged wing provided a good excuse for not shaking hands. Although it had been right dark that night, I felt sure he had recognized me. Still, I wasn't worrying any. I knew he couldn't get to pull his six-shooter fast, and I've yet to see a hombre of Devaca's caliber I couldn't outshoot. It developed that the man's name was Jake Strawn.

"Traveling far, Stephens?" he asked right off.

"Mebbe," I replied. "It depends on the hunting."

"Oh, so you're on a hunting trip, eh?" he sneered, and I knew he hadn't swallowed my story. "Must be you're after big game. I didn't see no shotgun on your saddle when I came in, and hunters don't usually pack two Colt guns and a pair of ca'tridge belts."

"Seeing you noticed that," I replied easily, "I won't have to explain to you that quail and rabbit — and coyotes — have no interest for me. I *am* after big game." Yeah, it was that extra six-gun that made my story sound phony, all right. I'd been against carrying it from the first, but after Santiago's buying it for me I didn't want to hurt his feelings by not wearing it. However, time was to prove that the old war eagle's hunch had been pretty sound, at that.

Again those sneery tones from Strawn: "Just what sort of big game are you after, feller?"

"That depends on a lot of things," I told him, then added meaningly, "While I'm after big stuff I'm not averse to knocking over a skunk now and then, should he get too inquisitive."

That shot struck home. I could see it in Strawn's eyes. I put down the spoon I'd been eating with and got ready for trouble. None came though. Strawn's face darkened like a thundercloud and he muttered, "No offense meant, pardner. I wasn't getting snoopy."

"Thereby," I shot at him, "proving you show good judgement."

Without another word he rose to his feet and left the house. Devaca, who had been listening to our conversation, followed him outside. I could hear them talking on the porch but couldn't distinguish the words. A few minutes later I caught the creaking of saddle leather and the sound of hoofbeats on the hard baked earth. That horse was being pushed plenty too; before I finished eating the sounds had died away.

I'd had a hunch that Strawn had departed to get some of his pals, so you can imagine my surprise when I rose from the table, said adiós to the woman, and sauntered outside to find him still on the job. He was seated on a small bench near the doorway, so I knew it was Pedro Devaca who had taken his departure. Mentally I shrugged my shoulders. One man was as good as another for carrying a message. That didn't make much difference. What the message may have contained was what interested me.

The instant Strawn saw me he got to his feet and, without even glancing at me again, started for the interior of the house.

I blocked his path. "Better not, Strawn," I told him. "I'm not aiming to have a flock of lead thrown my way as I ride off. I'll feel a heap better if you stay in plain sight until I've left."

"Who gives a damn how you feel?" he snapped.

"You'd better," I advised. "Because if I don't feel good you won't either."

His face flamed with anger, and he half stretched his left hand toward his holstered gun.

"Don't be a damn' fool," I told him, hard-voiced. "I could pull and shoot before your gun even cleared leather. You wouldn't want me to plug that other shoulder, would you?"

That tore things wide open: Strawn broke into a fit of cursing such as I hadn't listened to in many a day. It was raw and rough and made my blood boil. I suppose he figured I wouldn't take advantage of a wounded man. To tell the truth, he was playing safe on that score too. It was the first time his bandaged shoulder had been mentioned, but now he knew for certain who I was.

"You got a lot of guts, you have," he snarled when his breath ran short on cursing, "coming down here after what happened at the Golden Cactus."

I laughed at him then. "Meaning there's folks out looking for my hide to nail to a board?"

"That's for you to find out," he growled.

"I reckon," I conceded idly. "Well, if your pals are aiming to hang my skin up to dry they've sure got to move fast, became I'm figuring to make pronto time between here and the American border."

I wanted to give the impression that I was

headed north, so when Devaca returned with a gang of lead-slinging pals to get on my trail, they'd head in the wrong direction.

"Mexico or United States," Strawn rasped. "It won't make any difference. We're going to get you. Neither country will be healthy for the Gila Shadow — not with the reward that's hanging over his head."

Now I knew somebody in the gang had recognized me that night at the Golden Cactus. I didn't care much. Anyway, I couldn't see how it would make any difference. I smiled contemptuously at Strawn and looked him straight in the eye. Finally he commenced to shuffle uneasily. A lot of the rage died out of his face, and his glance commenced shifting around the horizon. Then I went on: "Strawn, if I ever hear of you trying to put me out of the way I won't be aiming at your shoulder when I catch up with you. Think that one over, my tough buckaroo!"

The threat worked better than I hoped. Strawn went the color of ashes. He tried to force a smile to meet mine, but it wouldn't work. "Hell," he muttered, "I can't do anything with a busted shoulder."

"I'm not taking any chances on that." My hand moved to his six-shooter, jerked it out of his holster. Then I sent it spinning through the air, throwing it as far as possible. It fell out of sight in some brush, quite a distance from the house.

I was expecting trouble from that move, but Strawn had sense enough to keep his mouth shut. I could see sheer hate burning in his eyes though, and I knew the Gila Shadow wouldn't last long if Strawn ever got things lined up the way he wanted them.

About that time I happened to think of Devaca's repeating rifle. I looked to the place where it had rested near the doorway, but the gun was gone. Devaca had taken it with him. There was certain information I should have liked to have forced out of Strawn — where Devaca had gone, who had been responsible for the attempt on Santiago's life, and so on — but even if Strawn had been in a position to furnish accurate details, which same I was inclined to doubt, I couldn't quite bring myself to put the pressure on him. Lots of times since then I've cursed myself for being chicken-hearted, but I never could jump a wounded man. Strawn was the stubborn type, too, and it would have required a certain amount of manhandling to make him come through with what I wanted to know.

And so I left him standing there near the

doorway, muttering curses while I went out to my horse, tightened the saddle cinch, and climbed aboard. "Adiós, Strawn," I called good-naturedly, turning the bronc away from the house.

"You can go plumb to hell!" he snarled, and I saw him turn and stomp back into the house.

It was nearly dark by this time, that sort of in-between light just after the sun has dropped behind the hills. The dusk lingered for another five or six minutes, it seemed, then night dropped down all at once. It wasn't long before the stars commenced to wink into existence. There was a soft breeze blowing, just hard enough to stir the grass tops. A good night for traveling, I figured. I glanced back toward the dobe shack once but could make out only a tiny oblong of yellow light shining from the open doorway. Even that passed out of sight a minute later as I reached the bottom of the hill and circled off to the left. My roan was traveling free and easy now.

10. POWDER SMOKE!

I pushed on steadily for about two hours. There were more stars in the sky now, and with them to help me lay out my directions

I kept heading south. I didn't have much idea just where to pick up Ramon Santiago's trail. All I knew was that he'd told old Pascal Santiago that he'd joined a rebel crew. That was my only clue, and it was up to me to get in touch with some rebels and, maybe, in that way eventually get news of Ramon. At that, I was still, more or less, going it blind, counting on getting a hunch or something of the sort to do something for me. Right then I had a hunch something was in the air, but I couldn't figure out just what it was. And I didn't feel so good about it either. You know how it is when you get a feeling that all isn't well but you can't dope out just what's wrong? That's the way it was with me. Howsomever, I didn't have much longer to wait to learn what was up, if I'd only known it. For that matter, if I'd known what was up I'd probably picked me a new direction right pronto.

The moon lifted above the eastern horizon before long. Being full, it made the country roundabouts almost as light as day. I was riding through hills spotted with hundreds and hundreds of those tall organ-cactus plants growing straight up out of tumbled slopes of broken rock. Right where the moon hit those slim columns it made a bright streak of light, and I was reminded for all the world of an army of soldiers marching up the hills with bayonets over their shoulders.

That strange hunch was bothering me stronger now. Automatically I shifted my right gun a trifle nearer the front and loosened my rifle in its boot. Twice I stopped my horse, got down, and placed my ear to the ground, thinking maybe I'd hear Devaca and his riders following me, but I couldn't make out a thing. The second time, just as I was getting to my feet, I caught a sound that seemed a heap like hoofbeats up ahead. I listened again, every sense tense, but nothing came of it, so I figured I must have been mistaken. I climbed to the saddle again, shrugging my shoulders and feeling like a nitwit. After all, I had no proof that Devaca was on my trail with a gang. It was just that hunch; that's all.

I was passing between two rocky hills when it happened. My pony stepped on a chunk of loose rock and slipped, momentarily throwing him off balance and jarring me to one side. At the same instant I felt the breeze of a bullet fan my cheek. Then from the hillside, to my left and above me, came the sharp crack of a Winchester. The horse slipping was all that had saved my life!

I'm telling you, I didn't lose any time getting out of my saddle. I was slinging lead out of my six-shooter before my feet struck the earth too. I hesitated just long enough to flip the reins over my pony's head so he wouldn't run, grab my own rifle from the boot, and scurry for shelter. My first shots as I left the saddle hadn't been intended to hit the hombre who'd thrown down on me — he was too far away for a six-gun to do much damage — but I did want him to keep his head down until I could get sprawled behind a heap of loose rock a dozen steps away.

Did I say a dozen steps? Mister, they were the longest steps I ever took, and I thought I'd never get there. But I made it, with flying slugs flattening on rock all around me. Once I'd flung myself down behind my shelter I reloaded my six-shooter, took a cautious look-see, and scanned the hillside from where the shots had come. There wasn't much to be seen for a moment, except a tumbled mass of rock and boulders sloping up to the crest of the elevation. I wasn't any too well hidden though, and I was expecting more shots every second. The slightest movement I made stood out plainly in that whitewash of moonlight.

Even while I watched there came a bright

stab of orange flame from the hillside. The bullet came close, too, and spat-flattened against a rock at my back. There was another big boulder not far from me, so I took a chance and ran for it, whining lead kicking up dust as I moved. Somehow I reached that new shelter without being hit. At that, it wasn't a comfortable situation to be in, with the thought in mind that Devaca and his gang might show up at any minute.

However, things were more nearly even now, so I threw my Winchester to my shoulder and cut loose with a couple of slugs. I knew the lead was just being wasted against rock, but I wanted to draw some fire and learn if my man had changed position.

He hadn't. In a moment his rifle cracked again, and I got him located. His bullet chipped off a chunk of rock close to my head though. Too close for comfort. That son of a buzzard could shoot! No getting away from that fact. Besides, he had the better position, too, being above me thataway, with a big boulder to hide behind. The moon made the night so bright, I could even see his shadow moving on a nearby rock from time to time. That helped a lot, because every once in a while when he shifted position I could see his shadow move in a way that warned me he was getting ready to shake some more lead out of his gun barrel. Once or twice I beat him to the shot, but I didn't have any luck scoring a hit.

Most of the time we were shooting close together. I'd see the flash of his rifle, then there'd be a momentary haze of powder smoke in the white night. By the time the echoes of his shot were dying away the report of my own rifle was carrying on the sounds. We took turns trading lead for the next half-hour or so. Neither of us was getting any results though. I was half afraid he might plug my pony to prevent me from escaping, but it apparently hadn't occurred to him. The roan was still standing not a great distance from me, though realizing I might need him any minute.

Finally I grew impatient of the game we were playing. Besides, I was curious to know who the hombre was. I decided to try something else.

"Hey, you, up on the hill!" I yelled. "Come into the open and we'll shoot it out. We're just wasting time — and lead — this way."

I waited a minute without receiving a reply, then repeated my words in Spanish.

This time I got an answer: "The plan is good, gringo," and the words were full of hate. "When I have counted three we will both make the appearance. Each man waits until the other has appeared, then we shoot at will. Agreed?"

"*Pues, sí,*" I called back. "Agreed, hombre."

I was plenty surprised, all right. In fact, you could have knocked me over with a feather. Here I'd been expecting to see Devaca and a bunch of riders coming after me at any minute, and it was Devaca who was doing the firing at me. He'd probably lain in wait a short distance from his hut, then, noting the direction I took, had moved on ahead to dry-gulch me. He'd picked a right likely spot for it too.

I waited an instant, then lifted my voice again: "The plan is good. Start the count, Devaca."

I'm admitting right now I was a double-danged fool to trust the bustard, but I did. His voice carried down the hill to me: "*Uno . . . dos . . . tres.*"

Taking him at his word, I stepped into the open, the butt of the rifle at my shoulder, ready to unloose a flock of lead the instant he appeared.

Without showing himself, Devaca thrust the barrel of his Winchester over the edge of his rock shelter and, aiming in my general direction, let loose a blast of lead as fast as he could pull trigger. I don't know why he didn't plug me. His bullets were coming close together. I heard a couple of them whine on either side of me, then I dived back for shelter without pausing to think how lucky I was.

I was mad clear through at the way the dirty oiler had tricked me. I should have known better than believe he would expose his own carcass to a hostile shot. The more fool me! I hadn't even fired a single shot. To make it worse, I could hear him laughing at my gullibility up on the hillside. He called down several jeering remarks. I didn't say anything. I had my rifle leveled, ready.

Finally curiosity overcame him. I guess he thought maybe he had winged me. His head edged warily around the corner of his rock shelter. Instantly I cut loose. It didn't do any good though. I was still so danged sore at myself for being tricked, I couldn't hold my gun steady. I missed by a wide margin. Then, in the hope of hitting him with a ricocheting bullet, I kept firing in his direction until my magazine was empty. All that brought me was some more scornful laughter. By cripes! Devaca had the most irritating laugh I've ever heard, and he sure made my blood boil.

I settled down behind my rock and commenced cramming fresh cartridges through the loading gate of my rifle. By the time I'd finished that I'd cooled down considerably. I told myself I'd have to think up something, or eventually Devaca would plug me before I got around to shooting him. This sort of business couldn't be continued. It was just a waste of time — a dangerous waste of time.

And then I got an idea. It wasn't too sound an idea, but still I figured it might work. Still I'd have to build up the idea in his mind first and give him something to think about, so when I pulled my trick it would look natural to him. Of course I might not be able to fool him. However, I figured it was worth a try.

I raised my voice again, speaking in Spanish: "Devaca, how long do you intend to keep this up?"

His reply came: "Until I have killed you, Señor Gila Shadow."

"I may kill you first, Devaca. In fact, I intend to do just that."

He laughed scornfully down at the sound of my words. "Gringo dog, you talk like a fool. I shall kill you, then take your horse. It is a very fine horse, or I should have killed it long since. And I shall receive many, many pesos as the pay for snuffing out your thieving existence."

That "thieving" part hurt. Still it was a matter of the pot calling the kettle black, so I let it pass.

Devaca was talking again: "I have all the best of the situation, Gila Shadow. I look down upon your place of shelter, and you cannot move from behind it without being seen. As for me, I move freely from place to place. My limbs do not cramp, as do those of one who remains in one spot. Do you note the difference?"

Yeah, I'd already noted that difference. He had all the best of it from that standpoint. I raised my voice again: "You overlook the fact I have a plan, Devaca. I shall continue to fire in your direction. I may not strike you, but my bullets, striking rock at your back, will rebound. One of them is certain to find its way to your miserable carcass — and the fight will be ended."

He was silent for a few minutes after that. I could almost imagine the wheels turning slowly in his thick head as he contemplated the proposition. I had him thinking all right, but I was still a long way from success.

Again I called to him: "That bothers you, doesn't it, Devaca? But it will be as I have told you. One of my bullets will rebound and strike into your body. Already I can hear your scream of pain as you leap upright and then fall from behind your shelter. Think, Devaca, can't you realize how it will be?"

I paused to let that sink in. I particularly wanted him to remember that part about the scream of pain and the leaping into view. Still he didn't reply. I shoved my rifle barrel over the edge of my shelter and let fly two quick shots. I heard them sing through the night and flatten against rock somewhere in his vicinity.

"Now do you see what I mean?" I called.

And now peal after peal of his contemptuous laughter came from the hillside. Apparently he was greatly amused — as I meant him to be. Finally he found his voice: "The plan is good, very good, Señor Gila Shadow. Only a fool would reveal his plan in such manner. But you have my thanks. The plan will work as well for me as for you. And already I have pointed out I am able to move about much more freely than you. Oh yes, gringo, the plan is good — as you shall learn to your sorrow!"

I caught the vicious whine of a bullet, then another and another. He was firing at the rocks behind me, and the flying slugs of death were rebounding all right. Luckily they were striking a sloping surface that caused them to fly upward. I sent a few shots flying on my own account. But I knew from the laugh that greeted them that he had already changed his position.

I figured I had him now. Let him keep up his firing for another five minutes, and my plan would be put into action. There was considerable low brush growing close to hand. I commenced swiftly to strip off my clothing while leaden slugs whined and screamed overhead.

11. Trail of the Big Cat

I was shivering plenty by this time. Lay it to the fact that I was standing in my boots and underwear and the night was cool. Or maybe the slugs whining overhead had something to do with it. Anyway, by this time I'd manufactured a dummy; stuffing my clothing with brush didn't require long. Hell, I didn't dare take too much time. The hardest part was making the hat stay on, but I finally managed that with the aid of a couple of whippy branches and some spines from a prickly pear. Now I was ready to go to work.

Devaca was still throwing lead as fast as he could fire and reload. To tell the truth, I was getting nervous about those flying slugs. One of them might find my body. I sent a couple of shots in reply over the edge of the shelter, then crouched low and took a firm hold on my dummy.

Zing, wham! Zing, wham! Zing-g-g, wham-wham! That last slug came dangerously close as it rebounded past my body. Abruptly I gave a bloodcurdling yell of pain, lifted the dummy, and tossed it from behind my barrier into full view.

If I do say it myself, I did a realistic job. That dang dummy landed right side up, hesitated just a moment, then sort of turned and slumped down, life-like — or death-like — as you please.

Then I crouched down below my shelter and remained silent. If I had known how to say a regular prayer I'd been saying one then. I waited, tense, wondering if the scheme would work. There were a few fleecy clouds in the sky now, passing across the moon. They didn't dim the light much, but they helped, I reckon. A minute passed. Devaca had ceased firing now. I waited, fearing every instant to hear that mocking, scornful laughter from the hillside. If Devaca gave me the laugh I'd know my fine plan was nothing but a fool move on my part. Worse, I wouldn't be able to get my clothing. And no man wants to put up a last-ditch fight in his underwear. There's no dignity in that.

Suddenly Devaca fired a single shot. I

heard the slug strike gravel after passing through the dummy. Then silence again. By God! I had him! He hadn't laughed and he'd fired into the dummy to make sure.

I didn't move a muscle. There wasn't another sound for a long time. The minutes dragged past. Probably I didn't wait long, but it seemed like hours.

Finally I heard a booted foot strike rock. I flattened out and risked a glimpse around the corner of my shelter. Sure enough, Devaca had left his place of concealment and was working his way cautiously down the hillside. I eased my rifle around to bear on him. From where I lay prone it was an easy shot. What is more, I was stretched in shadow from the rock beneath which I lay. He came nearer and nearer, stopping every few yards to listen. Each time he stopped I held my breath, fearing that the slightest movement would warn him I still lived. He was only about a hundred yards distant now. Then seventy-five. Then fifty. My rifle was cocked and ready. Glancing along my sights, I saw him as a clear target, nothing more. He was moving slow. It would be a cinch. My finger tightened about the trigger.

Then at the last moment I couldn't do it. Try as I would, I couldn't bring myself to shoot an unsuspecting man. Sure, I know, he had double-crossed me; he tried to murder me from ambush. There wasn't any call for me to treat him differently than he'd treated me. But, like I said before, I'm chicken-hearted.

I released the pressure on my trigger finger. Devaca was nearer by this time, his eyes intent on that dummy, his rifle held at ready in his hands. Abruptly he pulled trigger. I saw the dummy jerk to the impact of the bullet. Devaca hesitated, then continued on with more certainty in his step.

I was on my feet before he realized it, so intent was his gaze on that brush-stuffed dummy sprawled several yards distant from the rock behind which I'd been hiding.

"Perhaps, Devaca," I said coolly, "we'd better start that count again. *Uno . . . dos . . . tres.*"

A startled yell was ripped from his throat: *¡Madre de Dios!*"

That was all as he whirled about, facing me, shooting as he moved. I felt his bullet sort of pluck at the sleeve of my undershirt as it grazed past. My finger tightened about trigger. There was a spurt of white-hot fire. Powder smoke blurred the picture an instant. I heard Devaca's rifle clatter on the rocks at his feet. Then he spun completely around and crashed on his face. I knew a second shot wouldn't be necessary.

I didn't even bother to lever another cartridge into firing position as I stepped quickly across the intervening yards that separated us and, kneeling at his side, turned him over as gently as possible. Devaca's eyes were closed, but he was still alive. The crimson froth blowing from between his lips told me he hadn't long to go though. There was a dark spreading stain on his breast.

After a moment his eyelids fluttered open. His eyes were already glazing. "Water, for the love of God, señor," he moaned. "My lungs are on fire."

I rose and ran back to my pony, procured the canteen on the saddle, and returned to the dying man. I let a few drops trickle down his throat. His voice came a bit stronger. *"Muchas gracias, señor,"* he gasped. "Is it that I am to die?"

"I reckon so, Devaca," I told him. I felt sort of sorry for the poor cuss now, regardless of the fact he had tried to kill me. Shucks! I couldn't hold that against him. He'd only been playing the game according to his own code. At any rate, I'd had no choice in the matter; it was his life or mine.

His weakening gaze took in my underwear.

131

"You are . . . a very smart . . . man, Gila Shadow."

"Lucky," I corrected him.

"And I," he continued, "have lived . . . the very wicked life. Pray for . . . my salvation. . . ."

Right then I'd have promised the poor devil anything. I nodded and gave him another drink. I didn't want to press matters too much, but there were things I simply had to find out, if possible. "I see you recognize the Gila Shadow, Devaca," I said. "Were you of those who attempted the life of the Señor Santiago recently at the Golden Cactus?"

Devaca feebly shook his head. "No, señor. I had that story from Señor Strawn. In the beginning there were six men hired to accomplish that work . . . but it seems you arranged matters . . . you and two others . . . so more were required . . . for that affair. . . . Even so, they failed. You bear a charmed life, Gila Shadow. . . . El Gato would have had on hand . . . that night . . . even more of his men . . . had he known it . . . would be necessary ——"

"Who?" I broke in. That name had given me a start.

Devaca didn't reply at once. His eyes had closed. For a moment I thought he was a goner. I was wishing for a flask of whisky right then. Not having one, I trickled some more water into his mouth.

Devaca's eyelids opened slowly once more. He spoke with difficulty. "One called . . . El Gato Montés. . . ." he replied.

My heart was pounding like mad. Here was the first real clue I'd had, and I feared Devaca would slip off before I could learn the rest. "Quick!" I exclaimed sharply, striving to hold him together long enough for a few more words. "Tell me, where is El Gato Montés to be found?"

Devaca's eyes were shining like cut glass now. I knew he couldn't see me. His lips opened and closed two or three times, but speech wouldn't come. With his bandanna I wiped some of the froth from his mouth. He made a small gurgling sound; that was all. I knew he was trying to talk, but apparently he was too far gone. Finally, with my head close to his mouth, I caught one faint word, "Alzaga. . . ."

Alzaga! I knew the town. It was one tough community in any man's language. I might have known El Gato Montés could be found there. Even while I listened for further words Devaca's frame stiffened; a tremor ran through his body, and I knew he was dead.

I didn't wait long after that. I got into my clothing again. Just to keep the coyotes from messing around Devaca's body I heaped a pile of loose rock over it, knowing that Strawn, or some others, would probably come to see what had happened when Devaca failed to return. Then I picked up my rifle and went in search of Devaca's pony. I found it tethered up the hill a short spell behind a boulder as large as a house. Fastening the reins to the saddle horn, I gave the beast a slap on the rump and started it for home. A few minutes later I was climbing into my saddle again and headed south once more.

It must have been around midnight when I crossed a pair of railroad tracks. About a mile down the right of way there were some lights gleaming. It didn't look like much of a town from this distance, so I took a chance and wheeled my pony along the tracks.

Town, did I say? It wasn't even a decent-sized settlement. Just a scattered handful of dobe huts, all dark but one. The rest of the light I'd seen was coming through the windows of a small shanty standing at one end of a raised dirt platform. I figured the place served as a station for occasional train stops.

Santiago had asked me to keep him posted

if possible. This looked like the right place. Sure enough, as I drew near I could hear the *clickety-click-click* of a telegraph instrument. A few moments more found me entering the open doorway.

The round-faced young Mexican in charge nearly fell from his chair when he glanced up and saw me entering. Evidently he hadn't heard me ride up and dismount, and like as not he didn't know but what I might be a bandit. Aces to ten-spots I did look pretty hard to him, with my two cartridge belts crisscrossed at hips and a six-shooter filling each holster.

He wore an ancient train conductor's peaked cap, about five sizes too big for him, and he touched it nervously in a half salute after a moment, while his other hand reached to a drawer in his table — with the intention, I imagine, of getting a gun. I sort of grinned at him in that big cap, with his ears sticking out from the sides. He met my grin with one of his own and relaxed. "I am at your service, señor," he said politely. "You wish a ticket to Mexico City, perhaps?"

I shook my head. "Can you send a message for me, señor?"

"*Sí, sí,*" he replied eagerly, pushing a pad of telegraph blanks and a stub of pencil my way.

"I do not write your language," I told him. "Write down what I am about to tell you."

"Sí, señor."

I dictated in Spanish: "Hunting very good. On trail of big cat. Leaving for Alzaga at once."

When the words had been written down he read them aloud to me, then asked, "The señor is a huntsman, yes?"

"It is as you say," I answered.

I could see that the words "big cat" bothered him. I figured Santiago would know I meant El Gato Montés though. You see, I didn't want El Gato's name to appear for fear of arousing suspicions.

Finally the young Mexican thought he had caught my meaning. His face cleared. "Oh, you hunt the mountain lion — or the wildcat — no?"

"Yes," I answered.

"And one has been seen but recently?" He smiled.

"Many of them," I nodded. "But I wait for my *compañeros* to join me before making the kill."

"Sí, sí," and he laughed some more. In a minute we were both laughing and bowing and exchanging compliments like a couple of monkeys. I was anxious to get away, but in Mexico it requires time to transact busi-

ness. Maybe they've got the right idea, at that. But it was necessary that I first ask after the health of his family and if he prospered and how soon it would be before he owned the railroad for which he worked.

The questions were received in the same serious vein in which they were asked, answered with considerable exaggeration of facts; then we finished with the telegram.

"And to whom do you wish this addressed, señor?"

I wanted to keep Santiago's name out of the business, so I told the young Mexican to send it to Rug Wilton. Then I gave him the address of the P-Bar-S Ranch and told him to sign my name "Stephens."

"Can you send this at once?" I asked. I knew the message would go slow enough as it was, what with its having to be relayed and all. For that matter, I wasn't even sure it would go through.

The young telegrapher looked dubious. "There is so much of business, Señor Stephens" — he sighed regretfully, shaking his head — "I could not promise with certainty . . ." His voice trailed delicately off, as though hinting that the telegram might be put through, despite many difficulties, providing the right inducements were proposed.

I knew what he was after, all right, so I didn't hesitate. "For the sum of five pesos it could be transmitted by morning, is it not?" I asked.

His eyes lighted. *"Sí, sí, señor."*

"And for ten pesos — over and above the price of the message — it could be sent at once. Am I correct?"

His face was wreathed in beatific smiles. "You are *muy* correct. Ah, *válgate Dios!* Señor Stephens, for ten pesos — over and above the price of the message — I would myself deliver the words in person —"

"It is not necessary," I cut in.

"— but you understand, señor," he rattled on as though he hadn't heard me, "it is so necessary that I stay at my post, lest some evil befall the operation of this so excellent train schedule. Look you, I would not even accept your ten pesos except that my family is in sore need. I would make it clear, Señor Stephens, I do not take the money for myself, but when one's father and mother lack even the meal with which to make the tortillas, one is driven to extreme straits. . . ."

And so he rambled on and on, despite the fact he had informed me not ten minutes before that his father stood high in the government and that his mother spent all her days arranging grand balls for the Spanish nobility residing at the capital. I waited patiently for him to finish, then hinted, "Is it not best that you have someone send my message now?"

"I myself will send it," he announced grandly.

Of course I had realized that from the beginning, but he had to be urged by gentle stages. I stood over him while he clicked off the wire. A few minutes later, having paid him his money and after some further bowing and exchanging of compliments, I made my escape through the doorway and into the saddle.

Now I headed directly west toward Alzaga. I was feeling a heap better by this time. I'd come down into Mexico on what looked like a several weeks' — if not months' — search, and already I was commencing to pick up clues. What had at first appeared like seeking a needle in a camel's eye, or whatever that proverb is, was straightening out in a very satisfactory manner. Plain luck is my name for it. I reckon the gods were with me from the start. Not that getting a line on El Gato Montés meant I'd locate Ramon Santiago, too, but just the same, I had a strong hunch I was on the right track.

12. ALZAGA

It was a little over forty-eight hours later when the town of Alzaga hove into view. Sunrise was still a couple of hours off when, topping a rise of ground, I caught sight of two or three lights glimmering at the foot of a long slope, possibly two miles distant. It had been years since I'd visited Alzaga, and I'd sort of gotten off the track, or it wouldn't have required so long for the trip.

Nothing of any account had happened since I'd sent that telegram to let Santiago know where I was. I'd pushed my horse along as steadily as I'd dared, stopping only long enough, here and there, to snatch a few hours' sleep or grab a bite to eat at sheep outfits and stray huts on the way.

Now, with Alzaga before me, I hesitated, checking my pony's gait. I wondered just what the place held in store for me. In the old days Alzaga had provided a refuge for all the border scum that was slippery enough to escape the long arm of the law. Aces to tens, the town hadn't improved since I'd last put eyes on it. I wondered if El Gato Montés would be there — and if I'd get away from the place with a whole skin when the time for departure arrived.

To this day I don't know what prompted

the thought, but I pulled my horse to a halt and, taking one of my six-shooters, the Winchester, and the belt holding the rifle cartridges, I slipped down from the saddle and prepared to hide them. Luckily there were two blankets in my roll, and one of these served to wrap up the guns as a protection from moisture. At the last minute I added a handful of forty-five cartridges to the blanket. It required but a few minutes more to find a sharp chunk of rock with which to dig a shallow hole in the sandy earth at the foot of a cottonwood tree growing out there by its lonely in that expanse of country. There was lots of brush and rock around, of course, but that tree, standing up there alone, would make an easy mark to locate. A short time later the guns and ammunition were in the hiding place and the dirt stamped back over them. Then I scattered some loose earth and gravel over the spot and figured the weapons would be safe until I returned for them — providing I ever returned.

Climbing back into the saddle, I rode on with only the single six-shooter at my hip. I was wishing I knew exactly what lay ahead, though it was within the probabilities that I might be captured and disarmed. *Americanos* aren't any too popular in Mexico, anyway. At best, the chances were I'd be run out of Alzaga. When and if that came to pass I wanted some hardware where I could reach it easily.

It was just breaking day when I rode into the town. The sun hadn't yet lifted above the mountain peaks that marked the surrounding horizon, but the east was bright with crimson and orange colors. It was one of those pink-and-gold mornings. Cool, too, with a fresh breeze sifting through the hills. The sort of morning when steaming hot coffee tastes good and a fellow feels he's glad to be alive.

Alzaga wasn't what you'd call a large place in the States, but here in Mexico it was above the average, I reckon. Somewhere around eight hundred or a thousand population, I suppose. In short, a fair-sized collection of dobe houses, a few of them two-storied, painted pink and yellow and orange and white. Pretty muddy-looking colors at that. Some of 'em had tile roofs, others corrugated iron; some were thatched; others were of plain boards with earth heaped on top. There didn't seem to be any particular plan in the laying out of the town. Every man had built in the position that suited him best. However, there was a sort of well-beaten way that served for a street twisting between the houses, and along this thoroughfare I guided my horse.

Life was commencing to stir in Alzaga. A few chickens darted, squawking with panic, from under the hoofs of my bronc. At some of the doorways stood peons, serapes wrapped high around their faces, until only their sullen eyes stared out at me from under the brims of their ragged straw sombreros. In front of one hut a woman in a long loose dress that almost covered her bare feet pounded corn between two stones. Flies buzzed everywhere.

Smoke from the chimneys of many houses curled up to disappear in the turquoise-blue sky. At the time it didn't occur to me to wonder at finding the town astir so early or I might have known there was something unusual afoot. On the whole, though, I was feeling right good and not worrying a whole lot what would happen should I run afoul of El Gato Montés. With the day starting out so cool and fresh and bright, it didn't seem like anything could go wrong. And yet the sullen eyes of the people I'd seen kept intruding on my thoughts. When I stopped to consider that it didn't seem natural at all.

It took me a few minutes to notice that there were a lot of people heading toward the center of the town. Even then I didn't catch the idea; I just thought it was a fiesta day, or something of the sort.

And then as I guided my horse around the corner of a building a big open square spread out before me. On three sides of the square were shops and dwellings. On the fourth was a huge two-storied structure of dobe with the Mexican flag floating from one corner. That could mean only one thing: soldiers. That building was new since the last time I'd visited Alzaga — at least part of it was. Formerly the big building at that point had been a sort of general store and inn. Now it had been enlarged and was serving as a barracks.

Seeing the square filled with Mexicans brought me to senses. Something serious was afoot, no doubt on that score. The crowd thickened up, making further travel by horse impossible, so I dismounted, flipped the reins of my pony over a hitch rack before a *cantina,* and shouldered my way through the crowd. By the time I'd reached the inner rim of that mass of packed humanity I found myself within fifty yards or so of the barracks. In the wall of the building was a deep, arched entrance way opening on a big courtyard beyond. Across the entrance way was a pair of high, rusty iron-barred gates. The gates were closed at the moment, but seeing everyone's eyes turned their way, I watched those gates too. I was commencing to get a suspicion now of what was due to come off.

I didn't have long to wait. Just as the sun crawled above the hilltops and commenced sending waves of heat shimmering down on Alzaga I caught the high-pitched notes of a bugle. Right then the day seemed to change. The sun blazed hotter; the breeze died away. I could feel everything getting hot and stuffy and oppressive — sort of closing in around me. The peons in the square were feeling it too. Everywhere I looked nothing but sullen or sorrowful eyes met my gaze. No, they weren't liking this business at all.

Suddenly there were men at the iron gates which swung slowly open. Six soldiers filed out, marching two abreast. In their midst walked a seventh man with his hands bound behind him. At their head strode a dapper young Mexican lieutenant, cavalry sword dangling at his side. I knew what was coming now, but still, somehow, I couldn't believe it. Overhead the sky was blue and cloudless, clear as a bell. It didn't seem such things could be, and yet when I became conscious of the heat broiling down and the smell of packed humanity in that square and saw again the sullen eyes — well, I was wishing right then I hadn't been so curious; I cursed myself for pushing through to the front of that crowd. I turned back, but there was no forcing my way through now without creating a disturbance, so tightly were the people packed into that square. I'd have to stay and take it.

When next I looked the prisoner was standing against the adobe wall of the barracks, the six *soldados* lined up in front of him. Those soldiers made a ragged-looking group in their faded uniforms and bare feet. Only one of them possessed shoes. Their guns were of all lengths and makes.

The prisoner's face bore the look of a doomed man. He wasn't losing his nerve though. I sort of envied him his courage right then. He was a right good-looking young Mexican in loose white cotton clothing. The sun picked out high lights on his blue-black hair which had been neatly combed. By this time his hands had been untied. Back of him I noted that the wall was pock-marked with bullet holes, and there were a couple of dark stains on the earth near his feet. No, there wasn't anything new about this affair. It was a drama that had been staged innumerable times. That pock-marked wall was grim evidence of the fact.

The lieutenant moved nearer, spoke to the man about to be executed, then produced a packet of cigarettes. Each took one, lighted up, and stood chatting like good friends for a moment. Finally the lieutenant moved back a few paces and produced a folded paper which proved to be the decree of death. The lieutenant read in a loud voice from the paper. I gathered from the reading that the victim's name was Felipe Pueledo and that he had been sentenced to be shot to death on the charge of being a revolutionist. I doubt very much that Pueledo even heard the reading of the words. He stood calmly smoking, dark eyes flitting here and there among the crowd. For a brief instant an expression of pain flitted across his features as he saw someone he knew — probably a sweetheart or relation. The look quickly disappeared, however, to be replaced by a smile that was almost gay.

A hush settled over the square when the reading of the death decree had been concluded. I heard a woman wail briefly, then all was quiet again. The lieutenant spoke to the prisoner, his words sounding clear in the morning air: "If there is nothing you wish," the lieutenant was saying, "we will proceed to carry out the order of the government."

But Pueledo wasn't ready to die yet — not quite. So far the lieutenant had had his way. Now it was Pueledo's turn. He had his side of the story to tell. It didn't take long. He spoke in a clear ringing voice that fairly crackled once he was under way. There was a lot in the speech about honest people being under the heel of the oppressor and that sort of thing. The words took on an impassioned note as Pueledo outlined what had been his plans for his country and his devotion to the cause. One hand, the cigarette still held between his fingers, was outflung from time to time in a passionate declamation against all who disagreed with his politics.

I didn't hear it all. I wanted to jerk my six-shooter and take a hand in the proceedings — wipe out the whole Mexican army. I was too danged sore to listen to Pueledo's talk. But I realized I couldn't do anything; any effort I might make would prove fruitless. I couldn't save all the revolutionists in Mexico. Besides, I had other business in Alzaga. Just the same, Felipe Pueledo had all my sympathy at that moment.

A minute more and the speech was finished. Another breathless hush settled over the square, then, "I am quite ready, *mí Teniente*," Pueledo announced calmly.

148

The lieutenant bowed courteously, stepped back to one side of his men, barked out an order. Again I heard the bugle. The firing squad straightened. There was something pitiful in its earnestness. It didn't look like a squad of executioners; the men were more like a group of little boys playing at being soldiers in their ragged uniforms and obeying blindly the lieutenant because, for the moment, he represented the supreme command.

I couldn't help it; I closed my eyes for the moment. That didn't shut out the sounds though. . . .

"*¡Viva Mejico!*" came Pueledo's voice, a last defiant note placing an exclamation point to the words. There came another command from the lieutenant . . . then a ragged volley of gunfire.

I opened my eyes. Pueledo was still on his feet, something of a pain-twisted smile on his pale features, head up, hands open and slightly extended at his sides, the cigarette still held between fingers. Good lord! The firing squad couldn't miss at that distance, but it had. One or two bullets had struck but found nothing vulnerable. I commenced to realize the firing squad didn't like this any better than I did.

Pueledo spoke again. "I ask, my Lieutenant," he spoke unsteadily, "that you instruct your men to make more certain their aim next time, lest they find themselves occupying the spot on which I now stand." He spoke directly to the executioners. "It is all right, *compañeros*. Felipe Pueledo understands — and thanks you."

The words steadied the line of ragged soldiers. They looked shamefaced. The lieutenant spoke another order. I heard the click of rifle bolts. Once more Pueledo straightened himself, dark eyes steady on the rifle muzzles. The cigarette lifted to his lips for a last inhale. A vein of crimson coursed slowly from the ends of the fingers holding the cigarette. . . .

Again came an order from the lieutenant . . . the word to fire. The guns shattered the quiet. Pueledo stiffened, his eyes closed, but he remained erect. For a second I thought the firing squad had botched the job again. Then, quite suddenly, Pueledo's knees bent and he sagged limply down against the wall. Before the lieutenant could reach him Pueledo had rolled over on his back. A delicate wisp of gray smoke curled upward from his nostrils, tracing soft spirals against the blur of crimson.

The firing squad had again lowered its guns, slouched back to an easier position, and watched dully while the officer approached Pueledo, drew his holstered six-shooter and sent a final bullet crashing through the revolutionist's brain. The "mercy shot," they call it. After witnessing such butchery I could well understand why the mercy shot should be necessary. This was plain murder, no less. I can stand for seeing a man downed when he has a gun in his fist, but — well, executions are something mighty different; that's all. I don't like 'em.

I didn't want to see more. All through the crowd ran a subdued murmuring. Someone on my left mentioned there were still six others to be executed. Merciful God! My blood ran cold. I wasn't the only one who felt that way, either. There were muttered comments all around me to the effect that executions weren't popular.

"Ah, this El Gato Montés," grated one man under his breath. "He is a fiend!"

I wondered if the lieutenant was El Gato but felt almost certain he wasn't. The crowd around me had loosened up some by this time, and I could get through. I'd seen enough. Even as I worked my way back I heard the bugle sounding for the execution of another victim.

I caught other words on my way through:

— "they didn't offer him the bandage," a peon on my left was saying.

"Ah," came the reply of his companion, "that Felipe Pueledo was a brave man. He would never have accepted the bandage for his eyes. He faced the guns like a man, seeing them to the last ——"

"But, amigo, they might have at least offered it," was the petulant response.

I hurried on. What can you do with a people like that? They think more of the courtesies to be expected from a firing squad than they do the actual killing. But then, that's Mexico.

I was feeling sort of sick all over by the time I got back to where my bronc was waiting in front of the cantina. Only a short spell before I'd been thinking it was just the morning for hot coffee. Now coffee wouldn't do. I needed something stronger. I wanted a drink bad. Even as I was entering the open doorway of the cantina there came another ragged crackling of the guns from the plaza. Oh yes, I was needing a drink plenty by that time.

13. Gun Slinging

The cantina was a dim, low-ceilinged place with, at one side, a couple of tables and some straight-backed chairs. At the opposite half of the room stretched a rough board bar, behind which a fat bartender — he may have been the proprietor, for all I know — nodded in slumber on a tall stool, his back against the wall. There didn't seem to be any back bar to hold the bottles, though there were a couple of shelves with glasses on them. On the walls were a calendar and some pictures of bullfighters and a highly colored advertisement from a brewery. The subject was rather highly colored too. There weren't any customers in sight.

I rapped twice on the bar before the man in charge came awake. He must have been used to executions, because even as his eyes blinked open a rattle of firearms from the square fell on my ears. He gave no sign of hearing it though.

"The señor wishes something?" he asked.

"Tequila," I ordered shortly.

He grunted, maneuvered his fat carcass down from the stool, and placed a glass tumbler on the bar. Next he reached underneath for a bottle and poured a neat four fingers of the fiery liquor, after which he set before me a cracked saucer containing some salt and a withered slice of orange. I put some salt on my tongue, downed the tequila, and dragged the orange through my teeth,

Mex fashion.

The proprietor stood eying me sleepily.

I said, "There seem to be many executions taking place in your city, amigo."

That wiped the sleep from his eyes. I could see he didn't want to talk about the killings. Maybe he didn't dare to. His face took on a rather furtive expression, and he looked plenty uneasy.

"Would the señor wish another drink?" was all the reply I got, and I gathered Alzaga wasn't discussing its executions with strangers.

I shook my head. He replaced the bottle beneath the bar, hoisted himself, wheezing heavily, back on the stool, and closed his eyes. So far as he was concerned, the conversation was ended. He hadn't even waited for his pay. I dropped a coin on the bar; he opened one eye, muttered, "Gracias," and closed it again.

With a drink under my belt I commenced to feel a mite better. I even considered getting some breakfast, but I was still thinking about the way Pueledo had been shot down, and I wasn't sure if I wanted anything to eat. Queer how anything like that will affect a man. Seeing a hombre killed in a gun fight is a heap different from seeing him shot down without a chance.

I moved across the cantina floor and sat down for a while at one of the tables. Just how long I sat there, I don't know. From time to time I heard the bugle sound — always followed by the shooting of carbines. Finally men commenced streaming into the cantina, all talking in hushed tones, and I figured the executions were over for the day.

The proprietor — or bartender — was on his feet now, busier than a one-armed brand man with ticks. Twelve or fifteen men were lined at the bar. After a first glance none of them paid me any attention. There was a lot of talk about the shooting of the seven rebels, and once or twice I caught a mention of El Gato Montés, though no one was making any definite statements. They were all pretty cautious in their remarks and I gathered that the slaughter of revolutionists had been going on every day for a week or so.

I was about to rise and head out to the street when two men came blustering through the door. They were Americanos — I figured 'em as renegade cowpunchers from north of the line — and as ugly-looking a pair as you'd find in a month of Sundays. I could see they'd been drinking. Both were in flannel shirts, with corduroys tucked into their boot tops. Both packed six-shooters that looked as though they'd seen a lot of use.

The two of 'em pushed up to the bar, roughly elbowing their way between a couple of Mexicans, and called loudly for drinks. A sort of a hush fell over the place as the bartender served them. Some of the Mexicans put down their glasses and departed. Those who remained darted angry looks at the pair, though no one said anything.

I watched the two men closely. After a time I had a feeling I'd seen them before someplace. The more I thought about it, the surer I felt. That night when we'd rescued Santiago from the Golden Cactus I hadn't had much time to get familiar with the men who attacked us, but now I commenced to get a hunch the two at the bar had had a hand in the affair.

One of them was a burly brute whose nose had been broken at some time in the past. It had never been set properly, and there was a deep indentation across the bridge that sort of made it look like a saddle. His companion wasn't so heavy as Saddle-Nose, but he looked even meaner. He wore a very dirty canary-yellow neckerchief, and on his left hand were three cheap-looking rings. I heard Saddle-Nose call him Duke during the course of their conversation, which seemed to have to do with the executions of the morning. Once I heard the name El Gato mentioned but couldn't make out what they were saying.

I got to thinking I'd be in a mighty tough spot if those two had been at the Golden Cactus that night and recognized me. While I was wondering if I could take my departure without being noticed, Saddle-Nose turned and glanced my way. It was just a brief glance, but apparently it stirred his memory, for almost instantly he turned around and stared at me. Then he said something to his companion, who also turned for a look. The next instant they were heading in the direction of my table.

Now I knew I was in for trouble. At the same time I wasn't just sure what form the trouble would take. Maybe I could bluff my way out of a ruckus. I eyed the pair calmly enough as they stopped a few feet from where I sat.

"Ain't we seen you before someplace?" Saddle-Nose demanded.

"Maybe so," I said calmly. "I've been there a couple of times. I can't say you're familiar though."

"None of your lip, feller," the man named Duke growled. He turned to Saddle-Nose.

"Sure, I'm betting he's the same galoot."

Saddle-Nose nodded, then asked, "What name you packing, Mister?"

There was a sneer in his words I didn't like, but I wanted to avoid trouble right then, if possible. I said quietly, "The name is Stephens."

"Stephens, hell!" the other man exploded. "You're the Gila Shadow, or I'm a snake-eating skunk!"

"You don't need to explain," I snapped, getting sort of riled. "I knew what you were the minute I laid eyes on you."

"Skunk, am I?" the man snarled, one hand dropping to his holster. "By Gawd, I'll show you what's what!"

The gun was half out when Saddle-Nose interfered. "Shut up, Duke, till we find out a few things."

Duke dropped his gun back in his holster; I did the same. By this time the whole room was watching us, open-mouthed.

Saddle-Nose released his grip on Duke's arm and turned back to me. "We're aiming to learn a few things about you, mister," he stated meaningly. "Maybe Duke ain't so far wrong when he names you the Gila Shadow. If you are the Shadow" — and here he paused impressively — "El Gato's going to be mighty interested to learn you're here in

Alzaga — and pleased too. I'll bet he arranges a reception for you, one you won't forget as long as you live."

That struck Duke as funny. He commenced to guffaw; Saddle-Nose joined in, appreciating his own humor. The two of 'em laughed so hard they couldn't talk for a minute or so.

It was a nice mess for me to be in, wasn't it? Dang it, it was just my luck to run into a couple of El Gato's friends. I could imagine the sort of reception he'd arrange for me too. I'd seen and listened to those receptions in the square ever since I'd struck the town. Right then I figured the safest course was to make a break for my horse and get out of Alzaga plenty pronto.

"Look here, my belligerent bucks," I told the pair in no uncertain tones as I got to my feet, "you're barking up the wrong tree. I'm suggesting that you mind your own business! I don't know any Gila Shadow and I never heard of this El Gato. Does that satisfy you?"

Saddle-Nose and Duke sobered instantly. Duke started to swear, and his hand edged down toward his holster again. Saddle-Nose rasped, "No, it don't satisfy us. I've got a hunch you're the man we want. It's not necessary we should tell *you* who the Gila

Shadow is. And you'll meet El Gato soon enough. For your information, I'm relating that he's in charge of Alzaga right now. Oh yes, you'll meet him soon enough — too soon, I'm betting."

I laughed, sort of sarcastic, as though I wasn't worried at his words. "That being the case, I reckon I'll look up this El Gato right now and find out why his dogs come snapping at my heels when I come to his town."

"I figure you'll stay right here," Saddle-Nose growled in an ugly voice. "El Gato is out of town. He won't be back for a day or so."

That sounded good to me. The atmosphere in the cantina was mighty tense by this time. If I could only reach my horse out front I'd have a chance for a getaway.

Saddle-Nose and Duke figured they had me cornered — and I guess they did. But I've slipped out of mean corners before.

"There's good reward money to be collected on the Gila Shadow," Duke reminded his pardner.

Saddle-Nose laughed kind of nasty and nodded. I could see they were hoping I'd make a break for the doorway. For a few moments we just stood there, eying each other. My brain was working fast, trying to find a way out of the situation, but it sure looked like they had me trapped proper. In a tight spot of that sort, there's just one code to follow. Judge Colt laid down that code, and it's a mighty good one.

It wasn't necessary, but I gave 'em fair warning. "Listen to me, you hombres," I said, cold-voiced, "I'm aiming to leave here and I don't intend to be stopped — not by anybody ——"

That was as far as I got. Things started to happen. I saw Duke reach for his six-shooter. My gun was belching lead and flame almost before I knew it. I sort of lost track of the outside world after that. Everything was a mixed-up blur of powder smoke and orange flashes of fire and crashing shots that shook the rafters of the building.

All I had eyes for were Saddle-Nose and Duke trying to get their guns lined on me. Duke seemed to take a mighty long time to drop too. I felt the breeze of two of his slugs as they cut through the bandanna at my neck. Saddle-Nose had slumped at my first shot. He hadn't even got his gun clear out of the holster. . . .

Then things cleared a bit, but the room was swimming in drifting smoke, and the stench of burnt powder stung my nose. Both Saddle-Nose and Duke were down now.

Duke's body was all twisted, and he looked like an old suit of clothing someone had flung on the floor. Saddle-Nose looked queer, too, propped up on one hand like he was, with his mouth hanging open. There was a sort of dazed look of surprise on his face, and he seemed to be having trouble holding his head up. I heard the bump, finally, when it struck the floor. . . .

14. UNDER ARREST!

By this time men were cursing in frantic Spanish and fighting to get through the doorway to the street. Every one of 'em was scared out of a year's growth, I reckon. I could hear a Mex woman screaming outside, probably figuring her man had been bumped off. Faster than it takes to tell, the cantina was empty of customers. I was left standing by my table. There were two bodies sprawled on the floor. Behind the bar the proprietor — or he may have been just the hired bartender — had turned to a heap of ash-colored quaking jelly.

Maybe I could have made it right then if I'd pushed my way through the knot of figures struggling in the doorway. But my gun was empty. I didn't want to hit the street with an empty gun. It required only a few seconds to eject the useless shells and reload fresh cartridges into my cylinder, but those few seconds meant precious time lost.

I heard voices in the street. The next instant the crowd swept back from the doorway, and the lieutenant of the morning's firing squad came hurrying in, followed by six or eight soldiers. I could probably have emptied my gun and made a dash for it, but the odds were too great. Instead I dropped it back into my holster.

My arms shot into the air at the lieutenant's sharp command. One of the soldiers advanced and relieved me of my cartridge belt and six-shooter. The lieutenant glanced curiously down at the huddled, still bodies of Saddle-Nose and Duke, then he glanced at me, shrugging his shoulders. "The affair for those two," he said ironically, "seems completed. Tell me what happened."

Right then I got an idea that Saddle-Nose and Duke hadn't been popular with the lieutenant. He stood there, watching me, in his faded khaki, with a thin smile on his swarthy features. I commenced to feel a trifle better, though I guess I jumped at conclusions some.

"They took me for another man," I explained. "When I started to leave they drew their guns and were going to shoot me.

There was nothing left for me to do but _____"

The lieutenant's thin smile lengthened a trifle. "And you shot first?" he asked skeptically, one eyebrow raising a trifle. "Either they were of much tardiness in drawing their weapons or you were" — he hesitated — "of the speed of lightning — no?"

"I was lucky — fortunate," I told him. I tried to make it clearer with some further details.

Three or four of the patrons of the cantina had gathered sufficient courage to return by this time. They had all seen the affair — at least the start. One of them knew some English. They backed me up. The one who knew English talked the most. Yes, he had heard the quarrel, he told the lieutenant in Spanish. Yes, the señor who was still alive had been within his rights and had tried to avoid a quarrel. Of the shooting — oh yes, it had been started by the two who lay on the floor. They had received their just deserts, no doubt of that.

Here the fat proprietor — or maybe he was just the bartender — broke in with his story. He was glad that Saddle-Nose and Duke were no more. They did nothing but charge drinks for which they never paid. In addition they were continually annoying the young girls of Alzaga. Several others nodded eager assent to this last and added words that gave credence to my explanations. Half of them didn't know what it was all about, but by this time I could tell that Saddle-Nose and Duke were as welcome in Alzaga as an epidemic of plague.

The lieutenant listened patiently to the various stories, then turned back to me. "So," he said softly, "you are accused of being one known as the Gila Shadow. I have heard of him. Is it true, señor?"

"Certainly not," I denied indignantly. "I, too, have heard of this Gila Shadow. He is nothing but a holdup man. Do I have the appearance of a bandido?"

The lieutenant eyed me gravely. "That, señor, I could not say. Bandits look, I am told, much like other men." He shrugged his shoulders. "Two horses may look alike, but who is to say which has the heart of the killer until one saddles and starts to ride them?" He smiled a little and spread his hands deprecatingly. "It is difficult, I know, but how shall I choose? I have only your word that you are not the Gila Shadow."

"My name is Stephens — Dale Stephens," I said stiffly, trying to carry through the bluff.

"You have papers to prove that?" the lieutenant asked.

I produced my papers of identification and handed them over. He read them through carefully, then looked at me from head to foot. At last he said in warmer tones, "Your papers appear to be in order, Señor Stephens, but does a man go on a hunting trip with only a six-shooter?"

I was ready for that one. "I had a shotgun, Señor Lieutenant, but some rascal stole it from me while I slept last night. I came to Alzaga, hoping to be able to buy another one. This trouble was not of my making, so if you will return my papers and direct me to a shop that offers shotguns for sale I'll trouble you no more."

"I assure you, it is no trouble. I regret that you have been detained thus long. . . ." His voice trailed off into silence. Whether he believed my story or not, I couldn't tell. He appeared uncertain just what course to take. At that, he wasn't unfriendly. After a few moments he reached a decision: "To me, Señor Stephens, it appears a clear case of self-defense. Were mine the final word, you should be released at once, but I fear I shall have to hold you until the return of my *capitán.*"

"And your captain is —— ?"

"Absent from Alzaga at present. He is named El Gato Montés. Unfortunately these men you have killed were friends of El Gato's. It would be more than I dare to release you."

So there I was in another jam. The prospect wasn't cheering by a long shot. However, there was nothing to do but put on a bold face and make the best of it.

"You are not El Gato Montés then?" I said, more to make conversation than anything else.

"No, Señor Stephens. Allow me to introduce myself — Lieutenant Mateo Estabanez, at your service."

We shook hands on that. I could see from the look he had given me as he spoke the words that he wasn't overly fond of El Gato Montés. I could also see he couldn't realize just how serious the situation would be when El Gato learned I was suspected of being the Gila Shadow.

His voice was almost apologetic when he resumed: "I regret, señor, the delay, but be assured I shall make you as comfortable as possible."

"It is nothing," I replied as cheerfully as I could. "El Gato, when he returns, will probably view the situation in the same light as the honorable lieutenant."

"Quite so," he agreed, but I figured from his tone that he saw trouble ahead for me when El Gato got back. A minute later he said, "You will please accompany me."

Followed by the soldiers and some of the townspeople, we pushed through the crowd to my horse. I took the reins in my hand and fell into step at the side of Lieutenant Estabanez. The soldiers marched behind as we headed toward the square.

No doubt about it now: while officially I wasn't an actual prisoner, still I was being conducted with all the ceremony possible under the circumstances to the jail that adjoined the army barracks. Probably there are fellows, had they been in my boots, who would have chanced a leap on the horse and a dash out of town, but not this hombre. I'd witnessed one execution that morning, and while the soldiers' aim wasn't any too good, still the fact remains that bullets do kill — and seven men had died shortly after sunrise. Think that over, if you feel I was overlooking any bets. . . .

Estabanez and I were chatting like old friends by this time. I had to do a heap of lying about the number of quail I'd shot on my trip, and so on, but we were getting along fine. I commented on the executions. Estabanez' face darkened a trifle. It was a

168

cinch he didn't like that part of his job, though he didn't admit it in so many words.

"So many deaths are to be regretted, Señor Stephens," he murmured reluctantly. "But then, when El Gato Montés gives orders he expects to be obeyed. Two days ago he left with me the list of those to be — er — shall we say liquidated? Yes, that is it — liquidated. A very good word, in the circumstances. I have carried out the order to the letter, but now, thank the *buen Dios,* there will be no more executions until he returns to Alzaga. I get sick at the sight of so much blood." He risked a shy, sheepish smile in my direction. "Those are not the words of a soldier, you are thinking."

"The sight of blood only sickens when it is shed unjustly," I replied.

His face tightened a little at that. Perhaps he thought he had said too much. Again he shrugged his shoulders. "That is not for me to say. At any rate, what can you expect when there are so many revolutionists striving to obstruct government?"

I said boldly, "Maybe there's something wrong with the government, in that case — or at least with the underlings in authority who interpret the laws to their own advantage."

Estabanez glanced sharply at me. "Perhaps," he said softly, "you are not a huntsman, after all."

I smiled at him. "We were speaking of executions."

"Ah yes" — he nodded — "the executions. They are to be regretted, of course, but it is the fortune of war."

"But there's no war in Mexico," I pointed out.

"In Mexico there is always war," he gloomily reminded me.

At that, he was more or less right, I reckon.

We crossed the square a few minutes later, and the tall, iron-barred gates were swung open at our approach.

"I am sorry, Señor Stephens," Estabanez said again, and I could tell he really meant it, "that it is necessary to hold you. For myself, I have no quarrel with the Americanos. One of them once did my family a great service I shall never forget. I shall make your visit here as comfortable as lies within my power."

"Is a cell going to be necessary?" I asked, figuring his statement about Americanos was made merely to make me feel better.

But he would go no further, probably because there were too many soldiers near. "I regret," he repeated firmly, "that it is necessary to hold you."

I saw there was nothing to do but give in gracefully. I mentioned my horse and was assured that it would be fed and watered. A moment more and I had passed beneath the big arch, past the wide-swung iron gates, and into the courtyard beyond. The gates clanged shut behind me.

15. Rebels Are Always Shot

I'll say this for Lieutenant Estabanez, he did make me as comfortable as possible. I don't know where my horse and saddle were taken to, but my blanket and other duffel were brought to the cell they'd given me. Food and an olla of water were also brought in, and the man who brought them hinted that I could have a bottle of tequila for the asking. I didn't ask, mostly because I wanted to keep a clear head on my shoulders, but I gave the fellow the price of a drink for himself, for which he seemed very grateful. They hadn't taken my money, or Durham and papers, or any of my personal belongings. Excepting my six-shooter, of course.

The building — combination barracks and prison — was built in the form of a hollow square, with most of the square given over to the big flag-stoned courtyard within the four walls. The place was constructed partly

171

of rock and timbers, partly of adobe. Two-storied. The upper story, which had a narrow gallery with railing running around all four sides, was occupied by the soldiers' quarters. There weren't more than fifty men stationed there at the time. The lower floor had been converted into cells — probably seventy-five of them — opening on the courtyard. There were no windows in the back walls of the cells. The only light that entered them came through the stout wooden-barred doors facing the courtyard.

I occupied a cell in the south wall — heavy two-foot walls they were, too, the sort that would require a heap of time to dig through, even if the proper tools were handy, which they weren't. No, there wasn't any chance of my making an escape in that fashion. Mostly that first day I just sat on a wooden bench in my cell and cursed the luck that had made me mess up things in such fashion. I was commencing to realize I wasn't as smart as I'd thought I was. At the same time, I asked myself, just what else could I have done? It was a problem, all right; the half circle of brown-paper cigarette butts on the floor in front of my bench showed that I'd smoked a lot over that problem too.

From time to time through the bars of my cell door I could see soldiers walking across the courtyard. No two seemed to have uniforms alike; the same condition applied to the rest of their equipment. They were a rather poor, starved-looking bunch. Not that they wanted for food; I think, rather, it was a hunger for something else — home and a fireside, a woman and kids. Of course there were women about the town; a soldier's woman always follows wherever the Mexican army takes him, even into battles. But that's not like having a home with peace and security and the other things that go with a home. I've known those kinds of longings more than once. War and killings are bound to tie knots in a man's nerves after a time.

Estabanez had hurried off shortly after I was conducted to my cell. I didn't see him again until evening, shortly after my supper had been brought in. The sun was down now. I had just finished with my food and placed the dish to one side, when he appeared at the door of the cell, unlocked it, and entered. There were some small fires burning in the courtyard, and the light from their flames cast some illumination into the cell.

"Do you rest easy?" Estabanez asked when he had entered.

I grinned at him. "Finest hotel I ever

stopped at. Your apartments are plumb luxurious. I never saw such service, either. Matter of fact, I've been so comfortable I haven't felt like stirring out all day."

I caught the lieutenant's thin chuckle through the gloom as he fell in with my mood. "Should you care to have your boots polished, Señor Stephens, kindly place them outside your door before retiring. Perhaps you would like to have a rug of different color on your floor. Or does the color scheme please you?"

"It is perfect," I assured him. "There is, however — I hesitate to mention it — a shortage of implements; you might care to remedy the matter."

"Implements?"

"Just a small matter of a pickax and shovel," I said dryly. "I've always been interested in tunnel building. Or, failing the implements, perhaps you have an extra key about you."

"I shall take up the matter with El Gato Montés when he returns." Estabanez laughed. His laugh stopped suddenly. El Gato's name seemed to shrivel all of the humor out of the situation. I heard him sigh deeply. He drew out a package of cigarettes. "If you will permit me, señor," he said courteously. "It came to me that perhaps you lacked tobacco."

I was grateful for that. Not that I care for that black stuff they smoke down in Mexico, but it showed that Estabanez was doing his best to ease the situation. I accepted the cigarettes with thanks and invited him to a seat on the bench beside me. He dropped down and we talked for a time of one thing and another, our cigarette ends glowing in the darkness. I brought up the subject of my incarceration.

"I will do what I can, of course," he told me moodily, "but El Gato Montés is a hard man. He is the final word. He is in command here. Not that I want you to look on the dark side. Perhaps all will be well. It is only that I do not want you to hope too much. You understand, señor?"

I understood that I was in a damned tight jam, but I thanked him and told him I wasn't worrying.

"You have friends perhaps, in the United States, who will come to your aid?"

"I haven't got around to thinking about that yet."

Estabanez asked many other questions — where I lived, my business, how I happened to know so well his country. I could see that Gila Shadow stuff was still bothering him and that, in a polite way, I was being put through a sort of of third degree. I told him I was a cowman from Arizona who had recently sold out and was taking a little vacation.

Estabanez nodded when I had finished. "I do not wish to appear inquisitive, Señor Stephens, but you see I must learn about you all that is possible, so when El Gato returns . . ." The sentence wasn't concluded, but I could see he was preparing to present my case in the most favorable light when the time came. He continued after a moment, somewhat apologetically, "Revolution breeds fast in this part of my country. I feared for a time you might be here to aid those who rebel against the government. I wish to assure myself that is not so."

It was a delicate way of asking me point-blank if I was a revolutionist. Well, I thought I could clear his mind on that point. At the same time, if I wasn't a revolutionist, what was I? I felt fairly sure he hadn't swallowed my story about being a hunter. Perhaps, in the long run, it would be better to pose as a revolutionist, than have El Gato learn I was in Mexico on business for Pascal Santiago.

I laughed softly. "And what if I were a rebel, Señor Lieutenant?"

My laugh didn't draw one of his own.

"Rebels are always shot," he said in a hard tight voice.

"In that case," I replied dryly, "I have only the greatest admiration for the manner in which the current administration operates. I might even, if pressed, agree with El Gato Montés that the execution of revolutionists is the proper thing and will, eventually, prove of great good for the country's welfare. Of course you agree with me, and ——"

"Let's not make jokes about it, Señor Stephens," he requested heavily. "Already I have said too much. You know my feelings regarding these executions. But I can do nothing. I am a soldier, sworn solemnly to obey the laws of my country. Whether or not I agree with the orders given by El Gato is beside the point. I carry them out to his satisfaction. True, I could resign from the army. But I feel more may be accomplished by remaining ——" He broke off suddenly, already feeling, I guessed, that he had revealed more of himself than he had intended.

"Set your mind at rest," I said frankly. "I have no designs on your government." I added softly after a moment, "Can you say as much?"

He stared at me in the darkness, evidently

not trusting himself to speak. After a time his words came with difficulty: "The present situation is only a phase that will pass. Mexico, someday, will emerge to become a great power. . . . As for yourself, thank you for the assurances you have given me."

He rose from the bench at my side and said, "Adiós."

I noticed as he was departing that he left my cell door swinging open. Thinking he had forgotten it, I mentioned the matter. His teeth shone white through the gloom as he turned back. "I neglected to tell you, Señor, that you are free to go into the courtyard for a few hours each evening."

"You mean I can go out there — walk around?" I asked dumbly.

Estabanez nodded. "You poor fellows — the prisoners — must have air. The night provides that opportunity."

"You mean," I said, "that you let the prisoners out for a while each evening?"

"Sí, Señor Stephens — while El Gato Montés is absent from headquarters."

I followed the lieutenant through the doorway. "I should think you'd be afraid of someone making an escape."

"You forget, señor, that a sentry guards either side of the big iron-barred gates in the archway. That is the sole exit from this courtyard. My men are continually on the alert."

"If a friend on the outside," I speculated, "could reach the roof, a rope lowered into the courtyard might ——"

Estabanez' soft laugh interrupted me. "Don't get ideas, Señor Stephens, unless they are original. The rope-from-the-roof idea has already been tried — three times to my knowledge. Each time the friend on the roof was captured before he could aid the man he desired to rescue. They were both shot as rebels, you understand. El Gato likes blood." He added hastily, "That last wasn't said officially."

I caught the uneasy laugh that followed the words. "I've already forgotten you said it," I told him.

He nodded. "There isn't much time left. Walk out and get acquainted with your fellow prisoners. There are only fifteen or twenty remaining here at present. There will be less when El Gato returns. So make the most of a short acquaintance." The words were spoken lightly, but I knew the lieutenant's heart was anything but light when he thought of the executions.

Five or six small fires were burning in the courtyard when I stepped outside. The air had grown chill the instant the sun dropped below the horizon. Men were gathered in small groups about the fires, talking in low tones.

Estabanez lingered but a moment longer. "My soldiers will tell you when it is time to return to your cell," he announced, then hurried off and left me standing there alone. I could see he didn't want to appear too friendly — not with El Gato due to return in the very near future.

16. Doomed to Die

Lord, it was good to get outside again and look up at the sky. The stars were out — millions of them — shining down from the velvety black inverted bowl above my head. The air of the courtyard was fresh and clean after the stuffiness of my cell. There was a pungent odor of burning mesquite wood in the atmosphere. Somehow the place didn't seem like a prison where men were executed day after day.

I strolled round and round the courtyard, stretching my legs. I'd never before realized just how good freedom could be. Small fires were burning here and there; at two or three I saw prisoners playing with soiled packs of cards. Now and then I caught soft, carefree laughter. One man was singing an old

Mexican love song. No one seemed to fear what the morrow would bring forth. Each was living for tonight alone. Again, that was Mexico: *mañana* — tomorrow — will take care of itself.

Some of the soldiers mixed right in with the prisoners, too, and played their games and accompanied them in their songs. Everyone seemed friendly; no one paid me any attention. For a few minutes it was difficult for me to realize I was a prisoner. Then as I glanced toward the great gates at the archway I saw two sentries pacing slowly back and forth, carbines resting on shoulders. One walked just beyond the locked gates; the other was inside the courtyard. They glanced at me as I passed. Neither said anything, but right then thoughts of escape left my mind — momentarily, at least. I continued my walk.

It was on my fourth or fifth circuit of the courtyard that I noticed two prisoners huddled over a small fire in one corner. Both were talking low and earnestly. What led me to approach them, I don't know. Call it acting on a sudden hunch, if you like. That's as good an explanation as any. I was feeling the need of companionship about that time, and as these two weren't engaged in a card game, I figured I might as well get acquainted. They both looked up rather sharply as I drew near them.

"May I sit with you, señores?" I inquired.

With true Spanish courtesy they both got to their feet.

The bigger of the two replied politely, "Certainly, señor," though something in his tones made me feel I wasn't any too welcome. Right then I didn't understand why. Anyway, we all sat down about the fire — that is to say, I was on one side of the blaze, the other two huddled close together across from me, as though they didn't care to get too familiar.

The smaller of the pair hadn't opened his lips. I noticed he was a little more than a boy, though I couldn't see his features. Mostly I was judging from his height and slim build. At first he didn't take any part in my conversation with the bigger fellow, who was also young. The boy merely nodded his head from time to time and dropped his chin deeper into the serape drawn about his face.

I was finding it difficult to make conversation. Of course there was nothing but generalities to base our talk on — the weather, Mexican politics, cattle raising, one or two other subjects along the same lines — but the bigger fellow across the fire couldn't seem to get interested. He agreed with practically everything I said and only now and then put in a word of his own. I doubt if he even heard half my words.

I'll admit I got a big peeved at his attitude. It's a habit with us Americans to feel put out when our advances aren't accepted as we think they should be. Ordinarily I wouldn't have stayed beside their fire an instant longer, but, like I say, their manner was getting under my skin and riling me plenty.

I said, as sarcastically as I knew how, "Perhaps, señores, so much talk annoys you. Probably I should remain silent and allow you to make the conversation."

The boy didn't even reply, though I saw his dark eyes flash with irritation. I could see a slow flush run up the older fellow's cheek. "Your pardon, señor," he said apologetically. "My mind was occupied with other things. In our position it is difficult to maintain the amenities of polite discussion. Like ourselves you are a prisoner, no doubt, but it may be the charge against you is less serious. We, you understand, are charged with rebelling against the government, and ____"

His voice broke off. I cursed myself for a fool. Of course these two were rebels,

condemned to execution, doomed to die —
perhaps as soon as El Gato Montés returned. I should have realized they had no
time for a stranger — a gringo stranger, at
that. I got up, making apologies as I reached
my feet.

The bigger of the two was on his feet by
this time. His voice was full of contrition.
"No, stay, señor. I have acted very badly.
Steeped in our own troubles, as we were, I
was slow to realize you, perhaps, craved
companionship. The fault is all mine. Please
be seated."

Well, we sat down again. I remained, more
than anything, to keep from hurting his feelings. I still felt the boy would have liked it
better if I'd taken my departure. He sat
huddled across the fire, his eyes steady on
my face. Again I tried to make talk, but it
didn't go any better than before. Neither
the boy nor his older companion appeared
to enjoy my company.

I was growing more uncomfortable every
instant, with the boy's eyes on me all the
time, so I just stared right back, figuring to
make him look away. Probably two or three
minutes passed that way, with none of us
speaking and the boy and I just looking
steadily into each other's eyes.

Then something happened to me, something I hadn't expected. It struck me, solid and quick, like an uppercut to the jaw. With the firelight shining on the boy's eyes there couldn't be any mistake. I knew I'd seen those eyes before someplace. Where was it?

And then, as comprehension slowly dawned, it all came to me with a rush. I remember laughing a bit crazily. For a moment I'd thought I was having visions, or something. It couldn't be! And yet I knew. *I knew for certain?* Things were coming clearer now. . . . That night at the P-Bar-S when Santiago showed the photographs of Ramon and Paula. . . . No, I hadn't seen the boy's eyes before; I'd only seen a photograph of them. Besides, Paula wasn't a boy. . . .

My head was swimming like mad, but I managed to hold steady as I reached into a pocket and produced the packet of cigarettes Estabanez had given me. I offered them to the smaller of the two across the fire. After some small hesitation a cigarette was accepted. A slim, dirt-smudged hand reached to the fire for a flaming twig with which to light the tobacco. The tiny glare from the burning twig cast a red glow on the smoker's face. Say, I could have whooped for joy one moment — and cursed our luck the next. Remembering we were

185

prisoners sort of took the joy out of the occasion.

I offered my cigarettes to the other. He accepted one with a *"Gracias, señor."* I didn't have to wait for him to light up though. As he leaned forward to get the cigarette the dancing lights from the fire were thrown full on his face, picking out his features in bold relief. I knew then I'd found my man: Ramon!

I swung back to the other figure across the fire and spoke softly a name that had been close to my lips ever since I'd first seen her picture: "Paula. . . ."

The girl started suddenly, shrank back, and dropped her cigarette. The man at her side half started to his feet, then dropped back, tense, his eyes boring fiercely into mine.

"¡Poder de Dios!" he exclaimed. *"Señor,* what are you saying? Who are you?"

They were Pascal Santiago's daughter and son, all right. I'd never expected to find Paula down in Mexico too. No wonder I was bowled over for a moment. It was a shock to them too.

For the first time the girl spoke softly, and her voice was throaty, just as I'd known it would be. "Ramon — not so loud. Let us find out what this means."

Ramon nodded and sort of gasped. One arm went protectively about his sister's shoulders. She shook it off with a word of warning and glanced quickly around the courtyard. No one was paying any attention to us.

I spoke swiftly, low-voiced: "We'd better not speak in Spanish at all. Someone might catch a word of what we're saying. First, I came down here to find you, Ramon. I didn't expect to run into Paula too. This has pretty much got me stopped. You see, your father, Pascal Santiago, sent me ——"

"Sent you?" Ramon interrupted.

"To find you. He couldn't come himself."

"He is sick? He has been wounded?" Paula asked quickly.

I shook my head. "He's all right. There's nothing to worry about where he's concerned. I'll get all my facts lined up in a minute and give you the setup. . . ."

It took several minutes to get straightened out and make them understand I'd really come from Pascal Santiago. For a while it was just a muddle of mixed questions and answers. Ramon was plenty suspicious of me at first, and I had a *muy* tough time convincing him I was a friend. Not so Paula. Something — I don't know just what it was — passed between us in the first few moments after I'd called her by name and she'd recovered from her fright. We sort of clicked, if you know what I mean, and I knew the girl trusted me from start to finish. There was something more than just trust there too. . . .

I was mighty eager to get Ramon's side of the story and learn how Paula happened to be down here with him, but naturally they wanted to know about Pascal Santiago first, so I told what I knew; how I had met their father at the Golden Cactus, of the fight there, and how he had decided to send me in search of Ramon. I concluded by relating everything that had happened since I'd left the border line. Then I started asking questions about Paula.

A moment later I could have cursed with rage and disappointment: before Ramon or Paula had an opportunity to explain very much the guards came around to round us up and send us back to our cells.

Reluctantly we rose to our feet as the guards passed on to the next group seated about a fire. I said calmly, "Good night, señores," and walked off. Ramon replied in the same quiet tones. Paula didn't say anything; I reckon she didn't trust her voice right then.

A few minutes later my cell door was

slammed shut and the key turned in the lock by a guard, and I was left to my own reflections. Believe me I, was doing a heap of thinking as I dropped down on my cell bench and started to roll a brown-paper cigarette. One thing was lucky: they hadn't discovered that Paula was a girl. I could feel the hair at the back of my neck rising as the thought came to me of what might happen if El Gato learned she wasn't a boy. And yet, I could understand plainly enough why nobody had found out. Paula was sort of slim and boyish anyway. The old overalls and shirt she wore were miles too large for her and hung in huge shapeless folds about her slender form. The boots on her feet were large, heavy, shapeless things. During the day the cell was too dark for anyone to distinguish her features, and at night the girl kept her sombrero pulled well down and her serape wrapped about the lower part of her face, as is more or less customary with Mexicans. On top of that, she had kept her hands and face smeared with dirt. That helped a lot. Her black hair had been cut exactly like a boy's and had grown out enough to make her look like a feller who needed a haircut right bad. All in all, Paula's disguise was pretty complete.

I didn't sleep much that night. One minute

I was feeling happy over finding Paula —
and Ramon, of course. The next instant I'd
be plumb miserable. What could I ever
mean to a girl like Paula? Getting right
down to cases, I was nothing but a holdup
man, bandit, stick-up artist — call it what
you will. There was a bad record behind me.
Some people said I was hard-boiled. I
reckon that was true enough. You've got to
be tough, hard as nails, in a game like that.
Sure, I'd killed men. Thinking things over, I
was right glad it had always been done in
self-defense and that I'd always waited for
the other fellow to draw first. I had one
thing to be thankful for: I'd never killed
anyone on any of the jobs I'd pulled. The
only hombres I'd wiped out were men with
worse records than my own.

All anybody had against me were stick-
ups and stage holdups and bank robberies.
I'd never taken money from anybody who
couldn't afford to lose it. The hombres I'd
rubbed out had worse things than that
against 'em. No use going into details. Just
figure they were dirty skunks and let it go at
that.

But, just the same, I couldn't see where
the Gila Shadow had a chance with a girl
like Paula.

Besides, we weren't out of prison yet. Ramon had told me that he and Paula — Paula was using a man's name — were charged with being revolutionists. I remembered the lieutenant's words of only a few hours before: rebels are always shot. For a minute I couldn't breathe. My mind drifted back to that morning. Again I saw Felipe Pueledo standing against that pock-marked dobe wall . . . heard the ragged volley of gunfire . . . blood . . . and the mercy shot. . . .

When would their time come — Paul's and Ramon's?

I closed my eyes right, but it didn't do any good. I kept seeing pictures I didn't like. I'd see Paula marching out to that dobe wall with three soldiers walking on either side of her . . . then the soldiers with their carbines leveled . . . and the shots would start my ears ringing. Sometimes it would be Ramon I'd see being executed, but mostly it was Paula. Always there'd be the harsh tones of the bugle, then cracking guns . . . and an instant later the mercy shot. Somehow I could never picture myself in that role. Maybe that's because I was thinking about Paula all the time.

I nearly went crazy that night.

17. Sheer Nerve

Perhaps it sounds foolish, but when morning came I got one of the guards to bring me some soap and water and other things. I shaved! Maybe that's a laugh; I don't know. It didn't strike me that way at the time. I was aiming to look as presentable as possible, come nightfall.

Lieutenant Estabanez didn't show up all day, but a guard stayed close to my cell most of the time, and he made it clear I could have anything I wanted — within reason, that was, and not beyond the limits of the prison rules. Mostly I wanted three horses and a brace of Colt guns, but I knew it wouldn't do any good to request them.

That day sure dragged past slow. I thought the sun would never drop behind the hills. I could scarcely eat my supper, I was so excited. However, it finally grew dark, and the guards came around to let us out of our cells. I was probably the first prisoner to hit the outside air, then I pulled myself up short. It wouldn't do to show too much haste. I took my time and loafed around in the vicinity of my cell. There were several prisoners in the courtyard after a while; fires were being lighted, and greasy packs of cards were produced.

Taking a roundabout course, I ended up where I'd left Paula and Ramon the previous night. They got there about the same time I did. We couldn't show the joy we felt, but when I took their hands the grip they gave me was mighty satisfying. I noted that Paula's face and hands were clean, too, and I could see her red lips and clear olive skin and fine eyes shining in the light from the stars. Her fingers were long and cool and strong when they took my hand.

There were some mesquite roots still left by the ashes of the previous night's fire, and Ramon got busy and soon had a blaze going. We settled down, crosslegged, to talk, with Paula between Ramon and me. I got them to point out their cells. Ramon's was in the same block as my own; Paula's was situated across the courtyard on the opposite side. I noticed that after we were seated by the fire Paula commenced rubbing dirt on her face and hands, and she kept the serape up across the lower part of her face. I couldn't help thinking she'd taken that chance of being clean just on my account, and I was glad I'd shaved.

First off they both wanted to know all about me. I couldn't blame Ramon none for that, with me knowing about that silver that was hidden, and so on. Ramon had no way of knowing but what I might be one of El Gato's spies, and he wanted to feel safe before he talked too much.

I went over the whole story again and gave him a chance to check up on what I'd told him the night before. In addition, I outlined my past life for 'em: told them just what I was — all that Gila Shadow business. It wasn't any cinch; I didn't want to make a confession of that sort, but I knew I had to come clean for Paula. It had to be; that's all.

I reckon Paula must have realized how hard it was, because once her hand came across and rested on mine while I talked. She didn't remove it right away, either. Me, I was plenty ashamed of my past life by this time, but the touch of her hand made my story come easier. I got a certain amount of lift just from knowing she didn't turn against me.

They heard me through in silence. Neither said anything for a moment. I said, "Well, you know it all now."

Paula spoke promptly. "If you're good enough for Dad, Dale Stephens, that suits us."

"You suit us," Ramon said and shook hands again. I knew he wasn't holding anything against me. He looked more like his old war-eagle father every minute, and I liked him a lot. Ramon had produced an old deck of cards and from time to time, while we talked, he went through the motions of shuffling them. It made things look better that way.

Both he and Paula were taking matters mighty easy; they didn't seem frightened at the situation. Lots of nerve there, both of 'em. And I was so curious that I reckon I forgot to feel shaky.

"I'll be appreciating it," I said at last, "if you'll tell me just how Paula happens to be mixed up in this business. Your father, the last time I saw him, thought she was in school in California. So far as I know, he still thinks so."

Ramon frowned. "Paula was very foolish," he said. "She had an idea she could —"

"Ramon," the girl's throaty voice broke in, "it wasn't foolish. Or maybe it was. I don't know. I was only trying to help. At any rate, there's no use crying over spilt milk now. But if we hadn't got into this mix-up everything would have been lovely, I'm sure."

"Anyway" — Ramon shrugged — "there's no use arguing it all out again. Paula acted as she thought best in coming down here. That's all any of us have to go on — our own best judgment. We'll forget it. Hearing us rehash the matter isn't going to clear up matters for Dale."

I liked that "Dale." It was good to have them calling me by my first name — my own name. It seemed more natural, somehow, and I knew they'd accepted me as their friend.

"Suppose I start back at the beginning and give you details in their proper order?" Ramon suggested. When I nodded he went on: "Father told you that when the bandit, Pablo Vinada, robbed the Banco de Dinero he took the money to a secret hiding place in the hills and then killed the two men who accompanied him, so they couldn't reveal the secret. In that Father was only partly correct. Vinada shot both men, all right, but Father didn't know that only one of them died. The other was left for dead, but he recovered. I won't go into the whole story of how an old prospector found him wounded and raving out in the desert, but that was the case. He was an Americano, by the way, named Boyd, who had joined Vinada's band for the thrill he got out of such things as riding with bandits, and so on."

I wasn't so surprised at that. You hear of quite a few Americanos joining up with Mexican bandits from time to time. I had a chance to join Pancho Villa myself, once, but liked my own lone-wolf game better. I put in, "Pablo Vinada never knew this Boyd recovered, eh?"

"Vinada never even suspected it," Ramon replied. "Now comes the part about my meeting with Boyd. I'm a mining engineer, you know, and about seven months ago my firm sent me into New Mexico to look over some likely claims. I wasn't just certain how to get to the place, so the man who owned the property dug up this Boyd to act as my guide. That was how Boyd and I got acquainted. Up to this time Boyd had always been afraid to go back into Mexico; nor had he found anyone he cared to trust to help him get the money Vinada had hidden."

I nodded. "Naturally Boyd would have to be careful whom he took into his confidence."

"Boyd and I were together about a month," Ramon continued. "We got to be pretty good friends. He recognized my name, of course, and finally told me the whole story, including the robbing of the Banco de Dinero, the hiding of the money, how Vinada had shot him — everything. Boyd had settled down a lot by this time and was a pretty decent sort of chap. Even if he had played a small part in making trouble for Father, I couldn't hold it against him. It was the fortune of war, you might say; besides, he had been under Vinada's orders at the time, anyway."

Ramon paused while we lighted cigarettes, then resumed: "The sensible thing would have been to inform my father of the matter and let him handle it. However, I didn't. That's some more milk there's no use crying over. The upshot of the whole affair was that Boyd and I started down into Mexico to get that hidden silver. I had finished my report on the mining property, mailed it in, so I felt I was entitled to vacation. I realize now it was a fool thing to do. Neither Boyd nor I had given a thought of how we were to get the money out of Mexico. We intended to locate the silver first; the rest would come later — so we planned."

Ramon chuckled ruefully. "Most of the time since that day when Boyd and I rode across the Mexican border I have been in jail. We entered Mexico by way of Juárez. The first night we arrived there we were arrested as suspicious characters. There'd been a murder committed, and while the police couldn't prove anything against us, they held us in prison for over a month. We'd probably be there yet, except that the murderer was captured, and Boyd and I were released with many apologies. That has nothing to do with the story, except to show how I was delayed."

Paula cut in ironically: "Please notice, Dale, that I am the one who is supposed to have made the fool moves. Listen carefully and perhaps you'll realize such actions run in the family."

Ramon grinned in the light from the fire. "Shut up, Sis. Every man is entitled to his share of mistakes."

"I'm willing to bet" — Paula laughed softly — "that you've used up two men's quotas."

Those two had me stopped. Here they were in a mighty tight jam, but they could still forget their fix long enough to kid each other. I commenced to feel like a fool, worrying the way I had. I reckon I needed a little more of the mañana spirit — let tomorrow take care of itself when it comes.

Ramon continued: "Two nights later, after getting away from Juárez with Boyd, I made mistake number two. Boyd and I had arrived at a small town — Curales, I think it was — and I wrote a note to Father, telling him I was on the trail of the silver. That wasn't all. Now comes blunder number three: I waited there in Curales for an answer to my note, knowing Father would reply at once. While I was waiting a band of rebels swooped down on the town, and Boyd and I were captured. They gave us our choice of being shot or joining the band. What would you do? Sure, we joined the band; it looked as though it would be an easy matter to desert at any time. Besides, it gave us our freedom of the town. You see, the rebels — or bandits, as we later learned they were — didn't leave at once. They held the town for a couple of weeks, waiting for their chief to show up and join them. The town didn't much care who ran Curales, anyway. After the first night's excitement things went on pretty much as before. Father's reply to my letter arrived, and I again wrote him, saying I had been forced to join the rebels. Nothing looked very serious right then."

Ramon's cigarette had gone out while he talked. He leaned over to pick a flaming bit of wood from the ashes, inhaled a lungful of smoke, and went on: "The following day the rebel — or bandit — chief appeared. He was El Gato Montés —"

"What!" I exclaimed. "El Gato Montés?"

"The same." Ramon nodded. "The identical El Gato who commands this garrison and prison. Isn't it a sweet setup for us? He was a bandit then, and he's still a bandit.

His captaincy in the Mexican army merely serves to cloak his bandit activities. Right now he's on some raiding party or other — killing and robbing. One of the guards told me that in secrecy. El Gato isn't liked by most of the soldiers. To keep himself in favor with the government he makes a great show of picking up rebels and having them shot. It's been a slaughterhouse around here for a week now. By jeepers! I'd like —"

"Keep your temper, big brother of mine," Paula cut in quickly. "A temper is always bad for your blood pressure." A ghost of a chuckle permeated her words.

"All right, all right," Ramon growled, lowering his voice again. "But that's the way I feel just the same. El Gato is a bloodthirsty brute, and everybody knows it — even the government, I'll bet. Maybe it never hears the stories about him, of course. Or maybe it disbelieves them. But his soldiers know. Lieutenant Estabanez knows. But what can they do? El Gato would have them shot as traitors if they peeped a word, even if the government gave him his quietus later."

"You'd better finish your story, Ramon," Paula prompted, "if Dale is to hear it tonight. Our time grows short."

Ramon nodded and went on: "Let's get back to El Gato's arrival in Curales. Boyd

201

recognized El Gato the minute the man showed up at the town. You see, El Gato had had considerable to do with Pablo Vinada in the old days. And of course El Gato recognized Boyd as the man who had accompanied Vinada when the silver was hidden. El Gato realized that Boyd hadn't died, after all."

Ramon's voice grew bitter and his eyes hard. "To make a long story short, El Gato tortured Boyd to try and make him tell where the money was hidden. He had Boyd staked out on an anthill. . . . I learned later that Boyd was finished in half an hour, but he hadn't talked. My turn came next. Knowing El Gato from what my father had told me, I expected the anthill death too. However, I guess El Gato saw that business might not work. Of course I was searched, and from my papers El Gato learned who I was. And due to Boyd having been my pardner, El Gato was sure I knew the hiding place of the silver. He questioned me and questioned me. I denied, naturally, that I had any knowledge of it. I told him Boyd had never mentioned any hidden money to me. That's what I told El Gato. Boyd really had told me all about it — he gave me the location of the hiding place and all information. But El Gato couldn't make me admit that. And he couldn't be sure that I did know. Nor did he dare try to torture the information out of me: I might die the way Boyd had, without speaking. If I died El Gato never would learn the secret. He was wise enough to see that. And so he had me thrown into jail at Curales and left me there to think it over."

Ramon added half humorously, "And I thought it over plenty. I was half tempted to tell El Gato the whole business, but common horse sense prevailed. I knew he'd kill me once he knew the whereabouts of the silver. And I did want to help Father, if possible. One night my chance came, and I escaped from the Curales jail. El Gato sent men out looking for me, of course, but I was pretty well hidden up in the hills. For three days I stayed in the hills, then when El Gato's men gave up the search in the belief I'd made my way to the United States, I sloped down to a little sheep ranch that lay near by. The owner was an old man who lived alone; he was friendly and had no use for El Gato, so I told him my story. He agreed to help me return to the States. I didn't want to have Father run the risk of coming down for me, but I did need some money. I wrote a letter to Paula, explaining the situation and asking her to send me the money to get home with. I'd also promised the old sheepman some money. He mailed the letter to Paula for me, and we sat back to await the reply."

"And the reply arrived in due time, didn't it, Ramon?" Paula said, laughing a little.

Ramon said savagely, "Yes, dammit, it did! Look, Dale, here's what happened. Day after day that old sheep rancher made the trip down into Curales for the reply from Paula. I had told Paula to address the letter to him, you see. By this time El Gato and his thugs had left the town, but I didn't want to chance showing my face. But Paula's reply didn't come — not the way I wanted it. And then one bright morning I went to the door and looked out along the trail. You can imagine my surprise when I saw Paula riding through the gateway, leading a second horse behind her. I tell you, Dale, some women are so emptyheaded they don't know what danger means."

Paula just laughed some more. "You know it wasn't that, Ramon. I told you at the time I was afraid the money might not get through to you. Besides, I wanted the fun of the trip. You've no idea how stuffy university classes can become."

"You see," Ramon growled to me, "where there's no sense there's no feeling. You could probably stick her full of cactus spines and she'd never know it. She just didn't realize that Mexico is no place for a woman of her type. How she got through to me is more than I understand to this day. Bah! She wanted the fun of the trip. Paula had probably been reading a novel with a heroine that does everything a man can do. It went to her head. No, I forgot, she hasn't any head. But, imagine it, just a babe in the woods coming down here all by her lonesome —"

"That's not fair, Ramon." Paula smiled. "I wasn't a babe in the woods, as you say. I know as much about hunting and camping and riding as you do. Father saw to that. And I think I've managed to outshoot you on two or three occasions. You've probably forgotten; two summers ago I led a bunch of the university girls up into the high Sierras and we camped there all summer. And we managed to get along without a man."

"Yes, I know, I know," Ramon said scornfully. "Probably a great Boy Scout leader was lost to the world when you were born a girl."

Paula sighed. "You're a witness to the type of brotherly love I receive from this big mug, Dale. I leave it to your honest judgment — who has muddled things the most on this campaign?"

Before I had a chance to reply Ramon reached across and patted Paula on the shoulder. "Forget it, kid. I was only joshing. Frankly, I think you're pretty swell."

"On which high note we'd better call a truce." Paula smiled. "Time is short; time is fleeting. You'd better get on with the story, Ramon."

Ramon took up the thread of the narrative: "I still don't understand how Paula got through without trouble. But she was always lucky. Her luck was holding, I presume —"

"Of course," Paula cut in, "everybody was just lovely to me, until ——"

"Until we both ran into El Gato," Ramon finished. "But before that I figure that Paula had been fortunate in meeting the right kind of people here in Mexico — people who had helped her on her way. Honestly, it made me shiver when I saw her riding up to that sheep rancher's house that morning. There she was, all dressed in riding breeches, as though she were out on a morning canter in the States. There was no doubt about her being a gift. Well, I fixed that up mighty quick. From the old sheep rancher I procured the clothes she's wearing now, smeared some mud on her face and hands, and we started back toward the border line."

"And then," Paula took up the story, "it was just our luck to be picked up by El Gato Montés and his crew one night, just a few miles from here. And we'd been figuring we were making good time to the border, too, about that time. Anyway, the bandits cut us off; there was no way of escape. Thank the *buen Dios,* El Gato didn't take any interest in me; he was too pleased to capture Ramon again to bother about me after a first short glance. After they'd tied me in my saddle the band just ignored me. I'd given them a man's name, and they took me for a boy, of course. Then they brought us here. We're on El Gato's records as revolutionists."

"And I've been afraid," Ramon said, "that they'd find out, any minute, that Paula isn't a boy. I repeat, Paula, your luck is holding."

"I certainly hope so," she said, level-voiced, "but I suppose some bright morning they'll take us out against the wall and hold target practice — and from all I hear, the firing squads could do with a lot of practice. Oh well, there's nothing like feeling you're aiding a worthy cause."

I couldn't help admiring her nerve. There she was, death — maybe worse — staring her in the face, and she was taking it like a veteran, with a joke on her lips. She sure wore well, that Paula girl.

They were doing their best to make a joke of it, all right. Ramon said carelessly, "One nice thing, Sis — they'll probably practice on you first. I'll get a chance to learn if you can take it. El Gato's afraid to have me shot for fear he never will learn the whereabouts of that hidden silver. But that can't go on forever. He'll hold off as long as possible, of course, but eventually I'll get mine. He talked to me just before he went away. He was plenty peeved — told me he was losing his patience. I suppose I really should get ready to do my part in improving the marksmanship of the Mexican army. Oh well, we can't die more than once. What have we got to lose?"

The fire was dying down. I sat staring dumbly into the glowing embers, not able to say a word. What have we got to lose? Good lord! Courage ran in the blood of the Santiagos, no doubt about that. I've heard plenty of talk about American nerve, but mine was slipping fast, I'll tell the world. American nerve? Huh! Here were a couple of examples of Spanish backbone that had me backed right off the map. I was fair crippled at the thought I couldn't do anything. And I was plenty scared too. I consid-

ered the cool manner in which Paula and Ramon were taking it, and right then I came pretty close to hating myself.

Finally I stirred. I had to say something. I tried to hold my voice as careless sounding as theirs had been. I even managed a short laugh. "We won't worry about this," I said. "I'll be getting you two out of here in a day or two."

Ramon just stared at me. Paula gave a sort of gasp, then brought her tones back to level. "Pleasant news, Dale — but are you sure?"

"It's a promise," I declared. "I've got plan." God forgive me for that lie. The wasn't an idea in my head, but I sim couldn't let that girl down. Nor Ram either. I had had to say something ju keep my own respect with that pair of g sters.

"Tell us about it," Ramon urged. could see he found it hard to believ wasn't blaming him, either. I didn what to say next to back up the bl making. Then I got a break. I n guards rounding up the prisoners ing them back to their cells. I we interruption of our conversatio did take Paula away from me. feet.

209

"I wired your father where I was coming," I explained lamely, "and I've got two guns buried a couple of miles from here in a safe hide-out."

Ramon's face fell. "But — but Father can't come down here," he said dubiously. "Even so, how can we escape from El Gato Montés?"

"Our time's up," I replied. "I'll explain it all tomorrow night when we meet. Adiós."

"Adiós," came Ramon's puzzled answer, and I walked away, Paula's soft *"Hasta luego"* saying good night to me.

The guards had arrived just in time to prevent my telling more lies. I didn't want to do that, because I could tell from Paula's eyes she was trusting me a heap. I didn't get much sleep that night, either. . . .

18. EL GATO MONTÉS

t was the third day. I awakened early, after restless night, to the creaking of the big on-barred gates at the entrance way and a ried assortment of lurid Spanish curses. mebody wanted to get in, and he was giv- the sentries plenty hell for not moving ter. I had a hunch El Gato Montés had ved. I was right too. About an hour after finished my breakfast of goat stew and

tortillas, washed down with some muddy-looking liquid they called coffee, Lieutenant Estabanez arrived at my cell, an anxious look in his eye.

"El Gato has returned," Estabanez announced hurriedly. "*¡Cascaras!* What a temper that man possesses this morning. He is like a wild beast. Already he has sentenced to be flogged two sentries — simply because they did not move quickly enough to suit him in opening the entrance gates."

All this while the lieutenant was unlocking my cell. He went on as I stepped outside: "I tell you, Señor Stephens, this El Gato is a butcher! The buen Dios will yet punish him for his villainies. . . . But come quickly; he wishes to question you."

We talked as I hurried along at the lieutenant's side. Estabanez told me, "He has gone over your papers, and I have told him the whole story — placing events in the best light possible for you — but he is very angry at the killing of his two friends, Duke and the man you call Saddle-Nose. I have tried to make it clear it was a pure case of self-defense on your part, but he refuses to listen." Estabanez lowered his voice: "This Duke and Saddle-Nose were members of a bandit crew of El Gato's — a crew of renegade Americanos, half-breed Yaquis and poor Mexicans who do not realize what they do. You will mention nothing of this, of course, Señor Stephens, but I wanted you to understand the real reason behind El Gato's animosity."

"I've heard something of El Gato's bandit crew," I broke in.

Estabanez looked sharply at me, then, "I do not wish to be overly curious señor, but you weren't, by any chance, were you, sent to these parts by the Mexican government to investigate El Gato?"

I shook my head. "Sorry I can't help you out along those lines, *mí Teniente.*"

"You are more than a huntsman," he accused.

I smiled and shrugged my shoulders. "*¿Quién sabe?* Who knows? At any rate, I am not in the Mexican Secret Service and had I known I was to encounter El Gato I should have run the other way as fast as possible. So you see, your suspicions are unfounded."

Estabanez sighed deeply. "My wishes fathered the suspicion, I fear. But someday my government will rouse itself and act. Many complaints have poured in to the capital, relative to the activities of El Gato. Perhaps the government does not believe.

But if something is not done I, myself, Felipe Estabanez, will yet have a hand in the beast's undoing. That I swear! I am not surprised to learn that you know of his villainies. It is no secret here at the garrison. But for the present we can do nothing. At the slightest obstruction to his wishes he would have us all shot — after accusing us of treason." The lieutenant's brows drew together in a look of hatred, but he didn't pursue the subject further.

We crossed the courtyard and ascended a flight of steps running up to the long gallery that ran around the second story. I wondered if Paula or Ramon had seen me from their cells as I walked at Estabanez' side. Reaching the gallery, I noticed a few soldiers lounging here and there against the wooden railing. They looked curiously at me, but nothing was said as they saluted the lieutenant when we passed. A row of open doorways faced the gallery on all four sides. Finally, as we approached one doorway, larger than the others, Estabanez slowed pace.

"El Gato's quarters," he said, low-voiced. "Be cautious with your words, señor, and you may get off with a whole skin. Watch your tongue! El Gato is smoking marijuana cigarettes this morning. Always that is a bad sign. . . . Come on."

I'm admitting that my knees were shaking when we entered the room. "Señor Dale Stephens," Estabanez announced, saluting. "You commanded that I bring him before you, *Capitán*."

I looked and saw a huge, bull-like figure of a man sitting at a desk across the room from me. A window opening at his rear let in light. At a second, smaller desk in a far corner was seated an orderly. My gaze came back to El Gato Montés. I noticed he didn't raise his head from the papers on which he was concentrating but continued work as though Estabanez hadn't spoken. Estabanez and I stood there in silence for a full five minutes before El Gato gave the slightest indication he was aware we were in the room.

I had plenty of opportunity to look the man over. He was a huge hairy brute with a flat nose, repulsive lips, and heavy black eyebrows that met in a straight line above the bridge of his nose. Hard as a rock, I figured him — all solid bone and muscle. His coarse black hair cut a triangular slash across his narrow forehead. His hands were oversize, powerful, with fingernails almost imbedded in grimy flesh.

Once he spoke briefly to the orderly at the

corner desk. I caught a glimpse of El Gato's eyes. They were small, piglike, and red-rimmed. Cruel glints burned in their depths. God, how I hated the beast even then. The orderly rose, closed the door at our backs. I glanced at the man as he stepped past us. He seemed to be a smaller edition of El Gato, and I guessed he was one of the bandit crew. He gave me a nasty look as he returned to his desk, but I pretended not to see. As a matter of fact, it was El Gato in his soiled khaki uniform that held my interest. The uniform blouse was unbuttoned; the shirt beneath looked as though it hadn't been washed for months. Sweat rolled down El Gato's cheeks. I guess the shirt wasn't all that hadn't been to the laundry. The air in the room was strong, oppressive.

Finally El Gato glanced at the lieutenant and extended a paper with one hairy paw. "The list of the guilty for tomorrow's executions, Teniente Estabanez," he said in a harsh grating tone.

Estabanez' lips tightened as he stepped forward and took the paper. *"Sí, Capitán."* Again his hand came up in a brief salute. "Señor Dale Stephens," he announced a second time.

Slowly El Gato turned his little mean eyes in my direction, then he displayed twin rows of strong yellow teeth in a nasty smile. "So-o-o," he sneered, "this is the gringo rat, eh?"

It wasn't so much what he said that got under my skin as the way he said it. I didn't answer his words; just met his glance.

"Fool!" he thundered. "Don't you know enough to salute your superior?" His voice had changed to deep guttural tones.

Probably I'd have shown a heap more sense by saluting him, but I was commencing to get peeved. "I am a civilian," I snapped testily. "I am not in your army. It is not required that I salute you."

His face went purple. "It is enough," he snarled, "that you should salute when entering the presence of your superiors."

"I'll commence to think about that," I shot back, "when I find myself in the presence of such as you mention." I was getting madder every minute.

El Gato nearly choked. "*¡Diantre!* You dare to talk to me like that — me, El Capitán El Gato Montés! Ha! We shall see." With an effort he calmed himself and rose from the desk. "You shall be taught to salute, gringo pig!"

Right then, as he approached me, I could see one reason for his name. Light on his feet, he was — like a big cat — moving swiftly across the floor toward me with all

216

the grace of a dancer. It was almost unbelievable the way he handled his huge hulk. From the corner of my eye I saw Estabanez move forward, then check himself. He could do nothing, of course.

I should have realized what was coming, but somehow I didn't. Maybe I was half paralyzed at the sight of that big form closing in on me. El Gato halted directly in front, towering above me. "Comes the first lesson in the salute." He almost purred now, lips drawn back from his yellow teeth. "You raise the right hand — thus" — and his arm came up in a gesture to accompany the words — "and then —" He paused, and the next instant that ham of a hand descended with sudden violence. . . . I felt his open palm on my left cheek, and it hurt like hell!

The blow nearly knocked me off my feet. I staggered back a few steps, scarcely knowing for an instant what had happened. I was dazed, shaken from head to foot. Then comprehension swept over me with a rush and I saw red. *I saw red!* I was like a madman as I straightened up and went tearing into El Gato.

My left fist shot into his stomach. I could feel the muscle there, giving under the impact of my clenched hand. With a grunt El Gato bent nearly double — just in time for me to work the old one-two on him. My right swung to the side of his head. Again and again I hammered at him. Maybe if I hadn't been so wild I could have put over a knock-out, but I wasn't thinking of scientific boxing right then. I was shooting in blows any place I could.

El Gato was roaring like a wounded bull, more in rage than in pain, as he tried to avoid my pounding fists and get set for a few wallops of his own, but I wasn't allowing him any time for that. I knew I had to stay after him every minute and keep punching . . . keep punching. . . .

I heard the door at my rear open, and I knew the orderly had slipped out to summon help. I was certain it wasn't Estabanez. I could hear the lieutenant's voice through the ruckus trying to persuade me to stop, but he wasn't taking any part in the fight — unless you consider enjoying it taking a part.

Time after time my fists thudded into that huge carcass. El Gato should have gone down under the attack, only he was so big and strong I couldn't put it across. Round and round the room I followed him, shooting in lefts and rights, uppercuts and swings. He was doing his best to defend himself, and I knew I was hurting him at last — he was squealing like a stuck pig now — but, luckily for me, he didn't know the first thing about boxing, and I was beating him to the punch every time.

And then — then as I rushed him the width of the room — he tripped over his spurs and went down — down at last! I was boring in so fast I couldn't check my momentum. As he landed on his back my right foot crashed squarely into his ugly face!

Right then I wanted to turn my heel and grind that foul mug into a pulp, but something landed on my back. It was that damn' orderly again, come back to help his captain after giving the yell for help. Outside somebody was tooting madly on a bugle. I reckon the orderly had put in a riot call to the army, or something of the sort. I could hear heavy feet thudding along the gallery.

I shook off the orderly, who was clawing and scratching like a tiger, whirled around, and let him have it — right to the side of the jaw. A knockout that time all right. He went hurtling back through the open doorway and out on the gallery. I heard the gallery railing splinter as it crashed through and dropped him to the flagstones of the courtyard below.

El Gato was climbing to his feet as I turned back. I remember giving a yell of pure joy as I landed on his chest. All I wanted now was to finish him with my bare hands. I reckon I'd gone loco by that time. I don't know why my arms didn't get tired. I was feeling fresher every instant, and my fists were sure finding marks to shoot at. . . . Then that rush of footsteps came nearer; there were excited voices and half a dozen soldiers pitched on top of me!

We struggled and fought and clawed all over the room. Both desks were turned over, and I heard a chair crash to pieces. Things were all my way for a spell. No matter where I struck I seemed to find a face. The air was filled with grunts, groans, curses. The place was a madhouse. Somebody was laughing crazily too. It was a half sob, half laugh. It sounded queer as hell. I discovered all of a sudden it was my own laugh I was hearing. . . .

I was finally overcome through sheer weight of numbers. I couldn't lick the whole damn' garrison, or even a portion of it. I guess they thought I'd gone insane. Maybe they were right. Things quieted down a mite after a time, and there were four soldiers holding onto me. I was right tired by this time; my arms and legs felt like lead. Those soldiers didn't have much trouble keeping me under control.

El Gato was just getting up off the floor. I

couldn't help laughing at the sight. One eye was closed; he was a solid mass of cuts and bruises. His face looked like chopped beefsteak. His lips were cut and his nose mashed to one side. Oh, I'd given him a beating all right. Right then I felt good. El Gato's mouth was hanging open, and slobber and blood were running down his chin. His uniform was a mess. There were three or four teeth missing — maybe more. He was trying to curse, but the words were a meaningless jumble.

"El Gato Montés," I taunted him. "Mountain cat! Wildcat, eh? That's all wrong, El Gato. You get a new name. From now on it's — alley cat, polecat!"

One of the soldiers placed his hand across my mouth. My right arm was twisted savagely up between my shoulder blades. That took a lot of the fight out of me. I shut up. I didn't care much by this time. El Gato knew what it meant when I'd called him "polecat," and he realized the name wouldn't be forgotten for a long time — if ever. He glared at me from that bloody mask that had been his face. There were some more mumbles that were meant for curses, then he went to his overturned desk, drew out a drawer, and procured a forty-five sixshooter. He came back, standing close to me, the gun leveled straight at my heart. I could see the red-rimmed hate in his little pig eyes. His finger was quivering on the trigger. God, the round black muzzle of that gun looked big. I thought: Well, this is the end. I closed my eyes. Not that I was afraid to face the shot; I wanted to see and think of Paula as I remembered her when my time came.

I heard El Gato's voice again. I opened my eyes. He was slowly, reluctantly, lowering the gun, as though arguing with himself whether to shoot me or not. Suddenly he tossed the gun to one side — and I knew I was being saved for something worse than shooting.

El Gato managed to mumble out some more orders, and the soldiers took me out of the room. As I passed El Gato took a swing at my face. I let my head roll with the blow. It didn't hurt much. I reckon he was too tuckered himself to do much damage from that standpoint.

I was hustled down the steps from the gallery and toward my cell, a half-dozen soldiers marching on either side of me. Estabanez didn't even dare walk at my side this time. It would have looked too friendly. I was between the soldiers; he was up front, leading the parade back to my cell.

"When do we go into conference again, my Lieutenant?" I called to him, trying to be funny.

It didn't click though. He didn't turn his head. "I am sorry, señor," his voice floated back, "very sorry for you."

That was all. The words sounded darned serious too. I didn't feel so good all of a sudden. Not that I was regretting what I'd done. Not by a damn' sight!

Then I was entering my cell and the door was slammed and locked behind me. I was feeling right tired all of a sudden, and I held onto the bars in the door for support. Estabanez didn't say anything. He just stood there, looking at me through the bars after the soldiers had left. I could tell by the look in his eyes he wasn't holding it against me, the beating I'd given El Gato. It was only that I'd got myself in deeper than ever, and there was a sort of pitying look on Estabanez' face.

I tried to laugh it off. "It was worth it, Lieutenant. You've got to admit I messed that polecat plenty."

He didn't answer. Just shook his head, turned, and walked away from the door. I dropped wearily down on my bench and reached for my Durham and papers.

19. A Fighting Chance

I'd given El Gato a beating all right, but I wasn't in such good shape myself. Not that I was hurt, beyond two sets of badly bruised and cut knuckles, but my clothing was in shreds. My corduroys had come through all right, of course; my shirt had been torn from my body. Only part of my undershirt was left. There were scratches on my face and the back of my neck, but they didn't amount to anything. My muscles felt sort of sore and achy too.

Most of my trouble was mental though. I was worrying now how I'd be able to help Paula and Ramon. Thinking things over, I cursed myself for an idiot. I should have taken that slap in the face El Gato had handed me and not said a thing. I should have saluted him. Most of all, I should have kept my temper and acted respectful. If I'd done that El Gato might have let me go. Once on the outside I could have made some sort of plan to get Paula and Ramon out. Yes, I'd been a fool all right. And yet, on second thought, had I? No matter what I'd done to please El Gato, it is quite likely he'd had me shot eventually. My killing of Duke and Saddle-Nose stuck in his craw. Maybe I'd taken the best course at that. At least I'd had the satisfaction of giving the big brute a licking, anyway. And that was a lot in my mind.

At any rate, it wasn't doing any good to argue with myself. What was done was done, and it was too late now to remedy matters. I might as well make the best of what life remained to me. Mañana would take care of itself.

Within a short time Estabanez sent over some fresh water, soap, and a shirt of his own. The shirt fit kind of snug across the shoulders, but it was clean and I was glad to get it. After I'd washed up a bit I commenced to feel almost cheerful again. If it hadn't been for Paula and Ramon I wouldn't have given a damn. That battle with El Gato had helped me work off a heap of surplus energy.

After a while I noticed that soldiers were commencing to drift past my cell and glance in at me. Some of them were handing me real friendly smiles too. I didn't understand at first, then it came to me: they were all anxious to get a look at the Americano who had upset their captain and tacked the name Polecat on him.

Finally, after a couple of hours, Estabanez showed up at my cell door. He didn't come in though. We talked through the bars. I thanked him for the shirt. His face was like an undertaker's: long and grave looking. Finally he managed to force a thin smile.

"Don't tell me" — I grinned cheerfully — "that El Gato, the Alley Cat, has sent you with an invitation to dinner for me."

"This is no time for jesting, Señor Stephens," he replied, shaking his head. "I fear for your safety."

"That makes two of us doing the same thing," I said dryly, but even that failed to bring a laugh. "What's going to happen to me, anyway? Am I to be rubbed out this afternoon?"

"On the contrary. El Gato has given orders you are to be well treated. If there is anything special you wish to eat, or a bottle ——"

"Now who's jesting?" I asked. "You'll be telling me next that the Polecat has ordered a carriage and horses to be put at my disposal. You might as well tell me the worst, Lieutenant. You aren't softening the blow any by saying that El Gato has ordered I'm to be well treated."

"But that is true. It's a custom of his to treat his victims well before he puts them to some special end. It's part of the torture procedure, I suppose, dating back to ancient Aztec customs. They always feasted their victims before putting them to death."

"And what is my special end to be?"

"Do you really care to know?"

"Why not? I might as well learn the worst now."

Estabanez said somewhat reluctantly, "El Gato hasn't quite decided yet. He has three ideas in mind. One has to do with hot irons. Or he might have you bound naked on top of a cholla bush. Or you could be buried to your neck in the earth and let horses trample you. And then there is the Death of a Thousand Deaths."

"Staked out on an anthill, you mean," I said as steadily as possible. "It all sounds interesting."

"Look you, señor," Estabanez said earnestly. "My talk is no part of the torture. I want only to prepare you for what comes. I like this no better than you. But you must understand, your situation is a dangerous one."

"And will it do me any good to start moaning?" I asked.

Estabanez shook his head. "You Americanos! No, it would do no good. You are a brave man, Señor Dale Stephens. I admire your courage. I wish I might do something for you, but it is impossible. You must understand that. For today alone you need have no fear. Mañana will be different. But today is yours. Now if there is anything special I can bring you . . . ?"

"There is. Two six-shooters and a handful of cartridges."

Estabanez sadly shook his head and moved away from the door.

I dropped back on my bench and rolled another cigarette. My future was shaping up for me now. El Gato would round up his bandit crew, take me out in the open country someplace, and stage a Roman holiday with the Gila Shadow as the victim. El Gato wanted me to shuffle off a little at a time so he could watch me suffer. It didn't size up good at all. The more I thought of it, the less cheerful I became. If only I could have seen Paula and Ramon get safely away, I wouldn't have cared so much. I was still young, but I'd crammed a lot of action into my years, so that wasn't bothering me. After all, a man can't die more than once. Anyway, that's the way my thoughts were running.

A sound at my cell door interrupted these meditations. I glanced up. A young Mex soldier stood there, grinning at me through the bars. He was a nice-looking youngster, so I gave him a smile and said hello.

"Señor," he said, his voice just raised above a whisper, "don't you remember me?"

I didn't, of course. I got off my bench and came nearer the door. No, I didn't know him from Adam. Still, there was something sort of familiar about his face.

"Have you forgotten José Captalaz?" he asked.

Now who in the devil was José Captalaz? The name didn't mean a thing to me. I was racking my brains hard too.

"Cuidad Sonora," he prompted my memory. "Remember . . . five years ago? My mother was ill. We had no money. You gave what was necessary for a doctor and medicine, and she lived."

And then it all came back to me. I recollected the kid and his sick mother. I'd found them plumb up against it, down in Sonora City one time. And here he was, making a fuss about a few dollars. I knew I stuck around and helped him take care of his mother for a month or so. It wasn't anything worth mentioning though. I'd been playing hide-and-seek with some law officers and had had to have a place to hole up, anyway. Seeing the woman sick had made me uncomfortable and — well, I'd done what I could. That was all.

Sure, I remembered José Captalaz now. He stuck his fist through the bars and we shook hands. I asked him how his mother was, and he said she was all right, healthy, and so on. Yes, she still lived in Sonora City — very comfortably on the money he and his brother sent her each month. We made some more idle conversation. José explained that he hadn't seen me when I was brought in.

"Of course," he was saying, "I knew there was an Americano imprisoned here, but I gave it small thought. Then today you became famous throughout the garrison ——"

"Yeah, I know," I told him sadly. "I'll be famous tomorrow, too, but not for the same reason."

"But that is not so, señor," José said earnestly. "You do not know how many in the barracks are pleased at the beating you gave to that El Gato. Of course we dare not show our pleasure. Nevertheless, nearly everyone applauds your action."

"That's just lovely," I said grimly. "That applause will help a lot about the time El Gato is tearing off my head and throwing it in my face. It's all right, José. I'm glad I gave you and your pards a little treat, but it's all over now. There isn't any more. El Gato figures to hang up my pelt to dry ——"

"But, no," José protested earnestly. "It shall not be! I, José Captalaz, will see to that!"

He was serious as the devil about it too. I almost had to laugh at the thought of this young private in the Mexican army doing anything for me.

"Look here, kid," I told him sternly, "you keep yourself out of this business. El Gato would have your head for supper if he thought you were interfering with his plans. You just forget me. Besides, you couldn't do anything alone."

He shook his head. "But in this I will not be alone. I shall go tell Lieutenant Estabanez at once. He will help. For me he will do anything — anything!"

I laughed at that. "You'd better not bother Estabanez," I advised him. "He's been right friendly to me so far, but he can go no farther. He has to look out for his own skin ———"

"When he knows who you are," José broke in, "and what you have done for us, it will be different. Our mother's life is owing to you. Mateo Estabanez is my brother, you understand."

No, I didn't understand. Their surnames were different. I mentioned that to José.

José explained: "He is what you call the half brother in your country, señor. Different fathers but the same mother. It was Mateo's own mother, as well as mine, whose

231

life you saved. But, wait, I go to tell Mateo *instantáneamente!*"

And with that he dashes off to find the lieutenant.

I commenced to feel a little more cheerful. I couldn't see the sky very well from my cell, but I knew it was a heap bluer than it had been five minutes before. What made me feel good was the kid's remembering and wanting to do something for me. And all because I'd spent a couple of bucks on him and his mother. I tell you, the hombre who said, "Cast your bread upon the water and it will come back cake," sure knew what he was talking about. Still, I didn't know how Lieutenant Estabanez would take the news.

I wasn't left more than ten minutes in doubt. Estabanez couldn't get away from his duties any sooner. He arrived, unlocked my door, and came rushing into my cell as excited as a fireman at his first blaze. "*¡Madre de Dios!* Señor, why did you not tell me about it?"

He took just long enough to close the cell door behind him, then both his arms went around me. Damn this latin temperament, anyway! It made me feel plumb foolish, and I wiggled out of the clinch. "Hombre, how could I tell you?" I asked. "I didn't know you were any relation to the people I knew in Sonora City that time."

We both dropped down on the bench, side by side. "That is true," he admitted. "And I had no way of knowing you were the man who saved my mother from death. That time you gave another name. Always I have hoped to meet the man who ———"

"Forget it." I cut in.

"I will never forget it," he announced dramatically. "I was away on service at the time. I could not know of my mother's illness. We were all very poor ———"

"And I was glad to help out." I interrupted. "In return for the hospitality of your mother's house. We're all square. And that's all there is to it."

"We are not 'all square,' as you put it. I am still in your debt. But we are losing time. I must talk fast, or El Gato will be calling for me. At present he is drinking heavily and is deep in his cups, but one never knows when he will rouse to some fresh deviltry. . . . Señor Dale, tonight you are to attempt an escape. I will do what I can. The rest is in your hands."

I said, "That's *muy elegante*," then kept my mouth shut. I wanted to hear how it was to be accomplished.

First Estabanez drew from his pocket a

key which he gave me. It was a heavy iron affair, well worn. "This is the master key to all the cells. I won't require it again today. If I should need a key I can call the guard. He has the keys to the cells. . . . You'll have to unlock yourself after it grows dark and all is quiet. That you can accomplish by inserting your arm through the bars and reaching the lock. I think you'll have no trouble in that direction."

"All I ask is a fighting chance," I told him.

"You'll get that." Estabanez next drew from within his uniform blouse my six-shooter and cartridge belt. Say, I was as tickled as a kid with a new whistle to get that shooting iron back in my mitt. It was still loaded as it had been the day he took it away from me. I hid the gun under my blanket and strapped the belt beneath my shirt.

Estabanez continued talking: "Don't be too sure you are free yet, Señor Dale. Getting out of your cell is simple. Then comes the hard part. You'll have to use your own judgment in getting past the sentries at the gate. I can't help you there. I could give you the password, but they'd suspect you and raise an alarm. They are both El Gato's men; he stationed them there himself only today. I don't dare take them into my confidence, or they would betray me. That I cannot risk because of my mother, who needs the money I send her. So, as I say, I can't help you with the sentries on the gate. They are loyal to El Gato and hope soon to be promoted from lowly sentries to position of honor — as they think — in El Gato's bandit crew. All I do is furnish you the means of getting out of your cell."

"I'll find some way of getting past that gateway," I said confidently.

"Don't be too sure. At night those gates are locked. The sentry on the outside carries the key. The key to the cell doors does not fit the gate lock."

Even that didn't shake my confidence. "I'll get through someway," I repeated.

"Today," Estabanez went on, "I am sending my brother José away on a mission. However, he won't leave Alzaga until you have tried to make your way through the gates. If you are so fortunate as to get clear you'll find José, any time around midnight, waiting for you in the shadows at the northeast corner of the square. He'll have your horse."

I started to thank him, but he wouldn't listen. Rising from the bench, he started out. I caught at his arm. "Could it be arranged that you have José waiting with three horses?"

Estabanez swung back in surprise. Then I explained: "Two of my closest friends are prisoners here, Lieutenant Estabanez. I can't leave them behind."

He didn't want to refuse; I could see that. Still, he couldn't see how it could be done. I tried to persuade him but didn't meet with much success. Horses were scarce. The risk was too great. I could see his side of the argument, all right. He was running plenty of chance as it was. If El Gato should learn his part in the affair Estabanez would be shot as a traitor. Still I persisted in my request.

Estabanez had said no for about the dozenth time, when I decided to take a chance. "I want to tell you," I said, "that I'm the Gila Shadow — the holdup man Duke and Saddle-Nose accused me of being that day."

That brought a smile to his face. "I suspected that all the time," he answered.

He was regular, that Estabanez hombre. Seeing how he took the news, I went ahead and briefly outlined the whole story. I saved the part about Paula being a girl until the last.

That really shook him up. He sank weakly down on my bench, one hand sort of weakly pawing at the air. *"¡Socorro!"* he gasped. "A

girl here? No, no! It can't be. You don
mean it."

"I mean it, all right." After a few minutes
I got him straightened out. Estabanez asked
the girl's name. I gave him the name — that
of a man — which was entered on Paula's
record.

"¡*Poder de Dios!*" Estabanez groaned.
"That name is on the list of those to be
executed at sunrise tomorrow morning."

Mister, I really *talked* then. It wasn't quite
so hard to convince the lieutenant now. He
didn't want to see a woman shot. Nor did
he relish the idea of having to give the order
to the firing squad. I kept boring at him,
like I'd kept after El Gato; he was weakening fast now. Finally he agreed to have José
waiting with one extra horse.

That satisfied me. I knew horses were
scarce. I figured Paula and Ramon could
make their getaway, anyway. I'd take a
chance on picking up some sort of mount
once I was clear of the garrison gates.
started to thank him again, but he cut m
short:

"One thing more, Señor Dale. Before
leave, drop the cell master key on the ea
near the wall to the right of the big gat
will find it. Tomorrow, should you es
there are certain to be inquiries, and a

237

will be called for."

I promised to take care of that part of it, and he started toward my cell door.

"There's one thing in your favor, Señor Dale," he mentioned before departing. "When your escape is discovered El Gato won't be able to pursue you until he has gathered his bandit crew, which is scattered around Alzaga or in the hills near by. Only his bandits have horses; there are none for the soldiers." He held out his hand to me. "May you and the girl be very happy, Señor Dale Stephens."

I wasn't expecting that, but I reckon he'd guessed how I felt when he'd heard my story. Somehow, I couldn't find words to answer him. I just gripped his hand hard. He borrowed the cell key to lock me in, then passed it back through the bars.

The rest of the day passed pretty slowly. Estabanez didn't return, and it was many months before I saw him again. One square Mexican, he was, I'll tell the world.

José showed up at my cell door toward evening. "Mateo sends me to inform you that I will be waiting with *three* horses tonight, señor. He feared you might be so rash as to remain behind while your companions escaped."

That was right welcome news. "You'll be

sure to wait for us, José? It may take us some time to escape. I wouldn't want you to depart, thinking we'd failed."

"I will be waiting." José nodded. "El Gato thinks I am leaving on a trip to buy beef for the soldiers. That is true enough, but before I leave on that trip I shall wait for you and your friends — at least until daylight. May you be very fortunate tonight, señor. *Hasta luego.*"

About an hour later one of the guards brought my supper. He spoke a little English and wanted an opportunity to use it. "With the so-happy regard of the Señor Polecat," he whispered with a grin. "Theese job you do today ees ver' good."

"I'll bet this food comes with the Polecat's happy regards." I chuckled. "What's he aiming to do with me?"

"Tonight, nozzing. Tomorrow" — and his face was very serious — "will be ver' bad."

"That's what I'm afraid of," I told him.

The guard shook his head. "You are not fear. Ver' brave man, señor."

"That's something that will have to be proved. Where's El Gato now?"

"Ver' dronk. Is asleep. Tomorrow hees wake up weeth ver' bad hang-under. Too moch of tequila. But tonight he ees snore like the pig."

The guard passed my supper through the bars and departed, leaving me hoping that El Gato would continue to sleep through the night and that his hang-over in the morning would take all ambition out of him.

20. THE DASH FOR FREEDOM

When it grew dark the guard returned to unlock my cell. "Eet is lucky that El Gato sleeps with soundness, señor. Else the prisonairs would not be allow' the fresh air. Weeth heem return' here, all liberty is feenish."

"Maybe it won't make any difference to me after tonight," I said, stepping outside.

"Is true, señor." He nodded sadly and passed on to the next occupied cell.

It was dark now. The small fires were commencing to spring into being about the courtyard. I strolled around for a few minutes, then went to join Paula and Ramon at their blaze which was just commencing to lick at the mesquite roots. I had so much to tell them that I scarcely knew where to start. They'd heard about the beating I'd given El Gato, of course. It doesn't take long for news of that sort to sift through a cell block. But I had to give them the story firsthand. Paula really got excited when I told about the fight.

"I wish I could have seen it," she exclaimed breathlessly.

"Bloodthirsty little brat, my sis." Ramon chuckled.

From time to time other prisoners drifted past our fire and spoke to me. I reckon they wanted to get a look at the man who had given El Gato the works. They made me feel they were all appreciating the job I'd turned out. That lifted my spirits a lot too. After a time we were left alone, and I got down to the real news I had to offer. I told Ramon and Paula to forget the plan I'd mentioned the previous night. That was one way of side-stepping questions about the bluff I'd been putting up.

"I've got a better idea," I told them, and related how Estabanez and José planned to help us.

It was worth a lot just to see their eyes light up when they heard the story. Gosh, the way those two acted you'd have thought I was one of these heroes like you read about in books. Anyway, I told them to be ready to leave any time after eleven. I checked on the location of their cells just so there wouldn't be any slip-up. Time went by fast that evening; it seemed no time at all before the guards started rounding up the prisoners. Our little session was broken up, and we had to part — for only a few hours, we hoped.

Back in my cell once more the minutes really dragged. While I waited I got out my cartridge belt and buckled it about my hips. Then I changed the loads in my six-shooter. For all I knew, they may have been tampered with; I wasn't taking any chances of that. The cylinder of the gun spun free and easy under my fingers, so I figured the mechanism was in good working order. Then I sat down to wait.

I don't know how long I waited, but my imagination was going full tilt every minute. I was thinking about those iron-barred gates at the archway and wondering how I was to get past the sentries. That was a problem! And the more thought I gave to it, the farther I seemed to get from a solution. I rose and paced restlessly the narrow confines of my cell.

Now and then I glanced out into the courtyard. Here and there a tiny pin point of glowing embers marked the spots where fires had burned some short time before. At one side I could see on the flagstones of the court the yellow reflection of light shining from the soldiers' quarters on the gallery. Even while I looked it went out suddenly, but I could still hear movements from above: the scraping of a booted foot on the gallery floor, scraps of profanity, the harsh scratching of a match for a cigarette. Waiting like I was, with all else silent, those sounds seemed louder than normal. I guess my nerves were getting edgy. I know I was sort of tense all over, and it didn't require much of a noise to make me tighten up like a coiled spring.

Another hour passed. I noticed now the courtyard looked lighter. I knew the moon was rising. There'd been some clouds the past couple of nights — it was building up toward the rainy season — and I was hoping for the same now. But it was too early to tell yet. The sooner I could get started, the less light there'd be, but I couldn't start while the soldiers were moving about above.

It was the waiting for the sounds to stop that was getting on my nerves — that and the thought that I didn't dare wait too long. The less light there was, the better chance we'd have. I could hear noises from the town, too, but those didn't bother me so much. I knew the townspeople wouldn't linger about the square beyond the iron-barred gates in the archway; they didn't like the soldiers being there — especially when El Gato was back from a trip. That business

243

of so many executions was getting on their nerves, too, Estabanez had told me, and they ignored the garrison and its inmates whenever possible.

It seemed ages before all the sounds did die down and everybody had turned in. Occasionally a snore reached me from one of the cells or from the barracks above, but that was all. Just to make sure I waited about half an hour longer, though it was getting brighter all the time. Luckily the moon wasn't as full as it had been a week before.

Finally I took a long breath. It was time to start. It didn't take me long to get out of my cell. The lock was even easier to reach than I'd thought it would be. I remember it squeaked like the devil when I turned the key. It needed oil. Probably it squeaked that way every time, but I'd never noticed it before.

I paused outside my cell and took another deep breath. All was quiet, but it wasn't cloudy, as I had hoped. The courtyard seemed fairly flooded with light. Right then I was darn thankful for that gallery running around the second floor. It kept all the cell doors in deep shadow, so long as the moon was directly overhead. I'd timed myself about right. It was somewhere in the vicinity of midnight.

I probably stood there a full five minutes, just to make sure. From the plaza beyond the gateway I heard a couple of voices raised in a drunken song. Probably some of El Gato's bandit crew roaming around. The town had gone to its beds long since — I hoped. I glanced down toward the iron-barred gates where the guards were supposed to be pacing sentry duty. Neither one was to be seen at the moment, but I knew they were there. The plaza beyond was bathed in moonlight. While I watched, a drunken figure reeled across my line of vision, probably bound home from some cantina — or headed toward another one.

I paused a minute longer, then commenced slipping down toward Ramon's cell which was situated in the same cell block as my own; Paula's cell — hang the luck! — was across the courtyard, on the opposite side.

Ramon was at his cell door, waiting, when I arrived. I eased the key into his lock, turned it. The rusty hinges squeaked protestingly as the door was opened. My heart almost stopped beating at the sound. We waited, tense, silent, hugging the deep purple shadows beneath the gallery. Apparently we were the only ones who had noticed those squeaking hinges, for nothing happened.

Now came the hard part. We had to go to Paula's cell. It would have been quicker to cut directly across the courtyard, but with so much light that was risky. It was safer to follow the shadow of the gallery all the way around; in that way there was less chance of one of the sentries at the gateway spotting us.

Neither Ramon nor I had uttered a word since I let him out of his cell. He placed a congratulatory hand on my shoulder for a moment. That was all. Neither of us spoke as he followed me around to Paula's cell. I'd never realized before how far it was around that courtyard, but on this particular night it was a devil of a long ways, I'm telling you. You can't make haste when you're moving carefully — and we were moving mighty carefully.

Once we'd reached her cell, it took but a moment to get the door open. Paula's face looked mighty white in the gloom as she came toward me. She was steady as a rock though, and for an instant she placed both hands on my shoulders. It was mighty sweet, that moment, standing there and looking down into her eyes. They were shining like anything. I wished it could have lasted longer, but we had to keep going.

The three of us got started again, sneaking along in the deep shadows of the gallery toward the big iron-barred gates in the archway. Paula was creeping along right behind me; Ramon brought up in the rear.

Luckily those gates were in shadow too. Now came the hardest part of the escape: getting through that gateway. I paused a moment and whispered to Paula and Ramon. They nodded and took up positions behind the big post that supported the gallery overhead. I'd seen nothing of either of the sentries who were supposed to be guarding the archway; I had to locate them before I could take the next step. I went on alone, getting near the big gates now. . . .

I scarcely dared breathe, I was so afraid of making a noise that would warn the sentries. Where the devil were they? Inch by inch I crept forward. Still no sign of a guard. I moved on, silent as an Apache.

Suddenly I could make out the dim figure of a man just this side of the archway, sitting on the earth with his back to the wall under the gallery. His serape was pulled well up around his face; his hat was down over his eyes. In his arms was cradled a carbine. Suddenly it came to me he was fast asleep at his post.

The breaks in the luck seemed to be coming our way. It required but an instant to tiptoe up to him. Then the barrel of my six-shooter landed solidly on his head, the blow cushioned by his hat. Slowly he toppled over on his side without a groan. I caught his carbine as it fell and lowered it carefully to the flagstones. Well, that was the first sentry taken care of, anyway. I remembered the key to our cells and tossed it on the ground near the wall, as Estabanez had asked me to.

Suddenly there came a slight noise at my rear, and I whirled around. Probably my deep sigh of relief came all the way from my toes when I saw Paula and Ramon standing behind me. They'd witnessed the whole thing.

Ramon put his mouth close to my ear. "What next?" he whispered.

I didn't know, to tell the truth. The other sentry was beyond the gates, still to be disposed of. The gates were locked, and he had the key. If he happened to be asleep like his brother sentry, it might be difficult to rouse him without rousing the whole barracks. Then I had an idea. "Wait here for me," I told Ramon.

I stooped over the unconscious sentry at my feet, placed his hat on my own head, and wound his serape around my face and shoulders. Then I picked up the carbine. The next instant I was around the corner of the archway, standing against the gates. The whole archway was pretty well shadowed, but I could make out the form of the other sentry slouched against the wall, just the other side of the gates.

He was on his feet, but I reckon he must have been about half asleep, because he started suddenly at my step and brought his gun part way to his shoulder.

"*¿Quién es?*" he snapped, his voice sounding sort of shaky.

"Be easy, amigo," I replied genially in Spanish. "It is only I. Have you a match?"

He relaxed, grumbling, "One who smokes should carry his own matches."

Plainly he hadn't noticed the difference in our voices — maybe he was only half awake — and took it for granted I was the sentry on the inner side of the gates. He grunted and came closer to the gates, put down his carbine, and rested it against one of the crossbars while he fumbled in his pocket for a match. Meanwhile I had rested the rifle I held against the big lock that held the gates together.

Then as the sentry passed a couple of matches through to me, instead of accepting them, my left hand shot between the bars and seized the man by the throat. At the same instant my right hand jabbed the muzzle of my six-shooter against his middle.

He managed to give one frightened squawk of fear before I shut off his wind. Then to top that off, in my hurry I knocked over the carbine leaning against the gate. It dropped with a clatter that sounded all through the courtyard. As though that wasn't bad enough, it exploded as it fell. The hammer must have struck on a loose paving rock, I reckon.

Immediately from overhead I could hear men stirring to action. I knew they'd be hell to pay in a minute if we didn't get out of there plenty pronto. Ramon and Paula came running up behind me.

"Quick!" I ordered the sentry in swift Spanish. "The key! Unlock these gates!" Just to hurry him along I gave him another poke in the stomach with my gun. The noise up above was increasing all the time. Somebody — probably that blasted orderly — was bawling loudly for El Gato.

The sentry hadn't produced the key yet. Precious moments were flying. I was getting desperate. "Quick, hombre! Open these gates!"

Unconsciously I'd tightened my grip on

the man's throat and was shaking him savagely. He was gurgling and gasping for breath. I loosened my hold a trifle to let him catch his breath. "Unlock those gates pronto!" I snapped. "It's that or your life!"

The sentry was willing enough by this time, but he was so scared I was going to drill him he could hardly move. He managed to get the key out of his pocket — a big old-fashioned thing it looked like, in the dark — and shove it into the keyhole. I heard the bolt shoot back.

Ramon was already tugging on one of the gates. It was a stout, heavy affair, and it was all he could do to move it alone. Paula was helping. I could hear soldiers running along the gallery above now. El Gato's voice came bellowing through the night — cursing, giving orders.

Taking my gun suddenly from the sentry's stomach, I raised it and brought it down on his head. Working through the bars like that, I couldn't give him the wallop I intended, but he slumped down like a poled ox. That was all I needed. I seized the gate with Paula and Ramon, and it swung open. Paula darted through first, followed by Ramon and myself. I'd have liked to have pulled shut that gate and locked it, but I didn't dare take the time now.

The next instant the three of us were out in that moon-lit square, running like mad. Back of us I could hear the soldiers getting under way in pursuit. There were some shots fired, but the slugs didn't come any-where near us, thank heaven.

With Paula between Ramon and me, we dashed diagonally across to the northeast corner of the plaza. There must have been more of El Gato's bandits roaming around town than I figured, for men seemed to spring up from all directions. Someone yelled at us to stop. Back of me came the sudden roar of a forty-five. We were moving too fast to make good targets though, and I unleashed a couple of chunks of lead from my own gun, just to keep the score even.

The first time I'd crossed the square it didn't seem nearly so big as it was now. Lord, I thought we'd never reach the other side. I was thankful that Paula girl could run. She was showing both Ramon and me a clean pair of heels. As for me — well, I'd never covered ground so fast before my own life under my own power. I seemed to be fated to be always going places in a hurry with these Santiagos. Mister, I was sure hoping José would be waiting with the horses. If he wasn't, our goose was cooked — boiled, roasted, and baked! And maybe burned to a crisp!

By this time soldiers had come steaming through the archway and were getting their guns lined on us. My heart jumped up in my throat someplace when the bullets commenced whining past. That whole plaza was a perfect bedlam, but we kept on going. We didn't dare pause.

We were nearly to the spot we'd headed for when two big hombres came dashing out from between buildings, guns in hand. I figured 'em for some more of El Gato's bandit gang, like the hombres behind us who had been slinging their lead around. I could see these two getting ready to throw down on us, so I slung my gun, shooting low. The two of 'em crashed to the ground, bumping together. One of 'em got his gun into action though and threw a couple of slugs our way. Both bullets flew wide.

While this was happening a third man had come charging toward us. I hadn't seen him, but Ramon had, and he acted in time. He didn't have a gun, but I saw him leave his feet in a long, low dive, flinging his body sidewise as he moved through the air. His hurtling form caught the charging man at the knees. I heard a forty-five explode harmlessly in the air and knew one bandit who had been taken out of the play

253

in extremely neat fashion. The two of them struck the ground together, but Ramon bounced up, landing, catlike and running, on his feet. He'd scarcely hesitated in his stride.

I caught his low laugh as he sped along a few feet away, then his voice, "I never knew before why I learned to play football."

Paula's voice floated back over her shoulder, "Nice block, Ramon!"

And then we were out of the plaza, in the shadows. I glanced around, but there wasn't a sign of José.

Before I had time to do any swearing though his voice reached me: "Here, señor! Quick! The horses are waiting."

Thank God! I don't believe I ever heard such welcome words. José was standing in the gloom between two houses. Back of him were the horses. We ducked out of sight in the shadows.

José started to help Paula up, but she had already vaulted into her saddle. Ramon was up. So was I. It sure felt good to have leather between my knees again. I reached down and gripped José's hand.

"Better keep off the street, señor," he was advising me.

That was good sense. Soldiers were running past now. I suppose they figured we'd kept on running in the direction we'd been headed.

We waited a moment, tense in the darkness. José said, *"¡Adiós! Vaya con Dios, señor."* His form faded away in the gloom between two buildings. Soldiers were still running past in the street a few yards away. From somewhere I could hear El Gato bellowing orders mixed with obscene oaths.

Well, we were on our own now. I said softly to Ramon and Paula, "C'mon." We turned the horses and headed them off between houses, moving as cautiously as possible. By this time the whole town of Alzaga seemed to be aroused. Lights were springing up everywhere. I caught frightened faces peering from open doorways as we threaded our way through the back streets of the town.

At last only open country lay ahead. Somebody — either soldiers or bandits — must have caught a glimpse of us, because I heard renewed yelling some distance behind. But by this time we were clear of the town and riding like the wind. Alzaga drifted farther and farther to the rear. Paula was riding between Ramon and me. I knee-guided my pony, leaving my hands free to reload my gun. I didn't know what instant I might need it again.

Ramon called across to me, "Well, we made it, Dale."

"We're not all the way clear yet," I answered.

Paula put in, "If we can't win with a head start like this we deserve to be recaptured. Isn't that right, Dale?"

Their voices were as cool and steady as could be. I hardly trusted my own voice. I knew it was some shaky. I said to Paula, "I know dang well nobody is going to take you away from me again."

I saw her glance at me rather queerly in the light from the moon. Maybe I'd said too much. I was right, too, about my voice being shaky. I didn't try to say anything more right then. We raced on and on through the night. . . .

21. THE FIGHT AT THE WATER HOLE

After a time the horses commenced to move up a long gradual slope, and I knew we were nearing the place where I'd hidden the Winchester and my other six-shooter. A little farther on I spied the lone cottonwood that marked the spot. That's what I'd been looking for. I twisted around in my saddle and glanced back toward Alzaga. I could see plenty of lights back there now, but as yet I couldn't see a sign of a pursuit. I reckon it was taking some time for El Gato to get his bandit crew mounted.

Another three minutes and we'd pulled our ponies to a halt near the tall cottonwood. Paula and Ramon stayed in the saddle while I got down, found a sharp chunk of rock — probably the same one I'd used to dig the hole — and proceeded to uncover my cache. The guns were still there. I gave Ramon the rifle and cartridge belt that went with it. Paula got the other six-shooter and the extra loads I scooped up from the blanket. She put the cartridges in her overalls pocket and thrust the six-shooter through the piece of hemp rope that held up the overalls. I folded the blanket hurriedly, tossed it over my saddle horn, and climbed up, thinking that it was lucky that Paula knew how to handle a gun. I had a hunch we weren't clear of trouble yet, by a long shot. Then we raced on.

We were making good time too. The wind whipped into our faces, and the scenery on either side seemed to flow past in a smooth unending stream of brush, prickly pear, and low hills. Now and then one of us said something, though in that rush of wind it was difficult to talk. However, we managed to make ourselves understood when necessary. The moon was pretty bright over the country through which we were traveling.

Paula was riding at my left. She called my name.

I said, "What's on your mind?"

She answered, "A while back you made a statement to the effect that you didn't intend to let anyone take me away from you again. Just how did you mean that?"

That one stopped me. I couldn't reply for a couple of minutes. I sort of gulped after a time and tried to explain. "I meant El Gato would have one hell — a very tough fight on his hands before he captured any of us."

I saw her kick her pony rather violently in the ribs, and it spurted ahead some. She didn't say anything more. I wondered if she was mad at me. I reckon she wasn't though, because pretty soon she dropped back at my side again. She didn't talk any more though, not to me. She and Ramon exchanged some conversation, but at the gait we were traveling I couldn't catch any of it.

I wasn't craving to slow our gait any, either. I knew it wouldn't be long before El Gato and his gang would be hot on our heels. It looked like a long chase, with a hard battle at the end, perhaps. I knew we couldn't beat him to the border. Our only hope was to lose him and his gang some-place along the line — if possible. Alzaga was far to our rear now, but it was a long way to another town of any size where we might get help or appeal to the authorities. And I wasn't sure but what El Gato might overrule any decisions the authorities might render. El Gato Montés still had the author-ity of the Mexican army behind him. No, the whole situation didn't look so good.

The moon dropped lower and lower. Finally it disappeared altogether. A new dawn wasn't far off and I wanted to find a good hiding place where we could hole up during the day. Once or twice now I thought I heard sounds of running hoofs behind us, but I didn't want to lose time stopping and listening. I was right sure, without that, that El Gato was on our trail and riding the hoofs off his ponies.

My own pony was holding up fine, but I was getting worried about Paul's and Ra-mon's broncs. They were covered with lather. Their tongues were hanging out. No dodging the fact that they were nags. I knew though that Estabanez had done the best he could for us. For that matter, those two horses had too — and they were still doing it, though they couldn't hold out much longer without a rest and some water.

I remembered seeing a water hole on my way down to Alzaga, so I shouted my directions to Ramon and Paula and swung slightly toward the east. The night was pretty dark by this time. I figured if we had to make a stand against El Gato and his hellcats, a water hole would be a mighty good place for it. Any way you looked at it, the horses simply had to have water. . . . By this time I had to hold my own pony in so as not to run away from Paula and Ramon.

It wasn't much longer before we commenced to near the water hole. It was still dark as pitch; the eastern sky hadn't started to gray yet. However, I was trusting to my sense of direction even if the night was as black as the inside of a pocket, and I was right sure I hadn't got off the track.

The water hole was down in a hollow, sort of saucer-shaped piece of land, about a quarter of a mile in circumference. As we drew near my horse sniffed water and plunged on ahead. The other two were close behind me though. We struck the lip of that big saucer, running full tilt, and plunged down the slight grade.

And then, there in the darkness, I realized we'd run smack-bang into a body of riders that had halted there for a drink too!

It was too late to warn Ramon and Paula

to turn and run for it. They were right on my heels and they realized, as soon as I, I reckon, there was a bunch of horses ahead. We all pulled on the reins at the same time, trying to slow our broncs and turn 'em. Even while I was cursing myself for not having gone ahead and spied out the situation, I felt the butt of my six-shooter leap into my hand.

Under some circumstances that would have been a fool move too. We were outnumbered. The odds were too great to shoot our way through. Men were all around me now, and I caught a faint glint of light on moving gun barrels.

Somebody snapped, "Pull up and raise 'em high! Pronto now!" Then another voice: "Take it easy. There's only three of 'em."

My heart skipped a beat. That was cowcountry language, or I was hearing things. What's more, I recognized one of the voices — I thought. I could hardly hold the words steady as I asked, "Is that you, Lamp?"

Men were all around us now. I caught the answer, "Sure, it's Lamp. Who in hell are you?" Then Rug Wilton's voice broke in: "By the seven bald steers, it's Dale Stephens!"

"They're friends," I called back to Paula and Ramon, and to save my life I couldn't keep from trembling all over. The relief I felt right then was tremendous.

I slipped down from my saddle. Pascal Santiago was standing before me. He gripped my hand — hard. For a moment he didn't say anything, then: "What news, Dale?"

"Plenty — good," I commenced. I heard Paula cry, "Dad!" Ramon's greeting cut in on hers. That broke off all sensible conversation immediately. Everybody talked at once. Believe me, Santiago was plenty surprised to find Paula there. For all he knew, she was still in school.

Santiago had brought eight cow hands with him, in addition to Rug Wilton and Lamp Lamonte. There were a heap of questions fired back and forth for a few minutes. Finally I pulled off to one side with the punchers to tell my story. I wanted to give Paula and Ramon an opportunity alone with their father. When I had finished I asked a few questions. Rug and Lamp took turns answering.

My telegram has been delayed, as I'd half expected, but once it had arrived Santiago had gotten busy and organized a crew to start after me. They'd made good time too. Santiago was taking chances, of course, but he was so sure I'd locate Ramon that he'd felt the risk worth while. And of course, now with Ramon and the silver located, Santiago would be able to square matters with the Mexican government if anything did come up.

It was growing lighter even while we talked. Santiago, Paula, and Ramon came over and joined the rest of us. The old war eagle's eyes looked sort of moist, but he gave me a smile and another shake of the hand that really meant something.

"Ramon tells me you think El Gato Montés is following you," Santiago said.

"I'm right sure of it," I answered. "In fact, I figure him as due to show up any minute now."

Santiago gave a sharp-jerk of his head. "Good! We'll be ready for him. . . . I've waited a long time for this."

He commenced giving orders. We had a good waiting place down in that hollow, out of sight of anyone traveling the level terrain. Santiago sent one man up to the rim of the saucer to keep watch for the first appearance of El Gato and his gang. The rest of us were down below, ready for action when it came. A small fire had been started. A pot of coffee was on the blaze. Some biscuits and dry beef had been produced. All of the cow hands had water in their canteens; that

263

in the water hole wasn't so good, except for the horses. It was rather bitter, alkaline.

I ran my eyes over the group of punchers Santiago had brought with him: Randle, George Lee, Gregory, Wolcott, Tony Verdugo, Burton, Hartley, Jim Parshall. They were typical sons of the range: lean, rangy men with muscular jaws, keen eyes, and weathered faces. Everyone looked fit to whip his weight in wildcats. And Lamp Lamonte and Rug Wilton — well, I'd already seen evidences of how they worked in a skirmish. In addition there were Santiago, Ramon, and myself. That made thirteen fighting men. I was feeling good and confident that we could give El Gato's crew a darn fine argument when it showed up, regardless how many men the bandit brought with him. Even Paula, still wearing my extra six-shooter, was ready for action. Santiago hadn't even hinted she was to keep out of danger. That's fighting blood for you.

We stood around in small groups, talking, while it grew lighter and the sun commenced to push above the rugged eastern horizon. Santiago, naturally, was standing with Paula and Ramon. They called me over once to join them, but I figured they'd sooner be alone and have a chance to get acquainted again. Paula kept looking my way, but I pretended not to see. Just because I had helped them escape from El Gato was no sign they had to treat me any differently than the rest of the hands, and I wanted them to know I understood how matters were. Rug, Lamp, and I were together, talking. None of us said anything in particular. I guess we all had our mind on the fight that was coming.

The rising sun hadn't reached down into our hollow when Jim Parshall, the man on lookout at the rim of the water hole, called down that he'd just sighted a body of riders topping a rise of ground some distance away. We all scrambled up to where Jim was watching and dropped flat on our stomachs, but we couldn't see anything.

Jim Parshall said, "They've dropped down in a hollow now. You'll see 'em again in a minute."

Santiago asked from a few yards away, "How many were there?"

"At a guess," Parshall replied, "I'd say somewhere between twenty or thirty riders. We'll be outnumbered all right."

Santiago laughed shortly. "Outnumbered? Since when do coyotes outnumber fighting men?"

Parshall nodded in agreement. "You're

right, chief. I reckon we can take care of 'em."

I glanced at Santiago contrasting him with the night I'd first seen him at the Golden Cactus. Then he'd been wearing a dinner jacket and black tie; now he was in cow-country togs. Somehow it didn't make any difference; no matter what he wore they were the right clothes for him.

Santiago raised his voice again: "One thing, men, I don't want anybody shooting at El Gato himself. I'd like to take him alive, if possible. That means a lot to me. Dale or I will point him out when he shows up, so there won't be any mistake."

The men looked at one another. They didn't say anything. I wondered what Santiago held in store for El Gato Montés if he was captured alive. It sort of worried me for a minute. I was remembering now that Santiago was Spanish. The Spanish don't always have the same ideas for revenge as we Americanos do. Hell! I should have known better than to have let it bother me. I might have known that torture wasn't in Santiago's books at all. But still, like I say, I wondered.

There we were, strung along the lip of that hollow, just peering over the top, alert for the first sign of the bandit crew. I was

266

sprawled out between Lamp and Rug. I heard movements behind me. There were Paula and Ramon.

Paula said, "Get over on the nest and let Ramon squeeze in beside you, Dale."

Lamp and I moved apart. Ramon crawled in between us, bringing the Winchester with him. I looked at Paula. She held up my extra six-shooter she'd been wearing. "When your gun is empty" — she smiled — "you can use this. I'll stay here and take care of your reloading. Give me some more cartridges."

Talk about cool! That girl made the proverbial cucumber look like a hot dog.

Jim Parshall spoke again: "There they come."

The announcement wasn't necessary. We'd all seen the riders at the same time as they came tearing over the crest of another slope. It was all rolling country hereabouts. That bandit crew was really riding too; every one of 'em was quirting his pony like a madman. Leading them was El Gato Montés. Big as he was, his pony was carrying him a good two horse lengths ahead of the other riders. There was no mistaking him. He had a brilliant red serape wound about his shoulders, and the ends floated out behind him in the breeze.

I caught Santiago's voice, something

triumphant in the tones: "That's El Gato in the lead. The big man with the red serape. Riding that gray pony. Remember, men, I want him alive!"

Behind El Gato rode a couple of dozen hard-bitten border rats, their sombreros jammed down on their heads, bandoleers of cartridges slung over their shoulders. Every man carried a rifle and at least one six-shooter.

Santiago spoke again: "Give 'em a volley, but shoot high!"

I liked the old war eagle for that. We could have ambushed the bandits, but that wasn't Santiago's way of doing things. He was giving them fair warning that they had more than two men and a girl to contend with.

The bandits weren't more than two hundred yards away when we cut loose with our guns. The rim of the hollow was fringed with white flashes of gunfire.

There were sudden yells from the bandits as they sawed on their reins. Their ponies came to sudden, sliding halts that lifted the dust and sent gravel flying in all directions. El Gato sat high in his saddle, peering toward the water hole, uncertain what he had run into.

Now Santiago climbed to the top of the rim and stood erect. "We're waiting for you,

El Gato Montés," he shouted. "Bring on your *pelados* and fight if you have the courage. You and I are due for the reckoning!"

Even at that distance I could hear the savage curse that lifted from El Gato's throat. He gave one insane shout, "Santiago!" then turned and spoke to his men, at the same time lifting his own six-shooter.

A sudden burst of explosions filled the air. Bullets whined viciously around Santiago. He dropped down out of sight again, a thin smile on his lips. "This time, men," he said, "make your shots count."

We shook some more lead out of our barrels, some using six-shooters; those who had them were pulling rifle triggers, But already the bandits had wheeled their ponies and were scattering. They didn't make good targets. One man plunged from the saddle. That was our only hit. I think Ramon got him, but I couldn't be sure.

The bandits drew-off out of range. Now that they'd heard our fire El Gato had had an opportunity to judge the size of our force. I reckon he must have decided he had us out-numbered, because in a moment he gave the order, and the bandits came charging toward us again.

"Hold your fire until they come close!" Santiago exclaimed.

But that wasn't to be. The bandits suddenly swerved their ponies and commenced circling the water hole. Round and round they rode, Indian-fashion, firing as they moved past. Santiago gave more quick orders. Some of our men scrambled up and dashed for the opposite side of the hollow. Within a moment more we were pretty well spaced out around the rim. Ramon and I remained close, Paula was crouched down right behind me.

I felt her take the gun from my hand and give me another, fully loaded. I drew a bead on a bandit, thumbed one quick shot. I saw him fling up his hands and pitch to the earth.

The bandit horses were still circling us. The air was full of powder smoke by now. The guns cracked continuously. El Gato was doing his share of the firing, but true to Santiago's orders, no one was firing at him.

Two riderless horses were galloping around the water hole now. Then three. I took a quick glance around. None of our men appeared to have been wounded yet. Well, we were pretty well sheltered, and so long as El Gato and his crew didn't charge us, the advantage lay on our side.

A slug whined dangerously close to my side, and I glanced quickly around at Paula.

Powder grime was by this time added to the smudges of dirt on her features. Her teeth shone whitely through the darkness of her countenance. "The hornets are very bad today, señor." She laughed.

Nope, you couldn't beat that girl for cool nerve. I glanced again at the bandits circling our hollow. I could count only eighteen now still in saddle. Some bodies were sprawled loosely on the earth by this time. I saw three riderless horses galloping off to one side. I don't know what had become of the other mounts whose riders had dropped.

There came a lull in the fighting. The bandits had drawn off, out of firing range. We could see them surrounding the big figure of El Gato, holding some sort of conference.

Rug called to me from a few feet away: "I reckon they don't like our dish, nohow."

Ramon said, "They're probably figuring to charge us in a body. It's their only hope. We're licking them at this rate. If only more of us had Winchesters ——"

"Horses, men!" Santiago's commanding voice filled the hollow. "El Gato is planning a charge. Get into saddles, but keep down, out of sight. Lamp, you stay where you are, let us know when they get nearly here. Then give the word. We'll do some charging on

271

our own account. Rug, you bring up Lamp's horse for him."

The men ran to get into saddles. In a moment we were all mounted and ready. I told Paula she'd better stay back. She gave me a scornful glance. Ramon chuckled and said, "I told you she was a bloodthirsty little brat, Dale."

Lamp's voice reached us from the rim of the hollow: "Here they come — and they're coming fast!"

"Come on, men!" Santiago shouted. "Give it to 'em — hot and heavy. But save El Gato for me."

With the punchers yip-yipping and guns roaring, we came charging up out of that hollow. The range was still too far for six-shooters, but I guess the shooting helped along the general effect. We reached the top and came pouring over the rim. Not two hundred yards away El Gato and his bandits were approaching, riding fast. Then they stopped — plumb sudden — and turned their ponies.

All that shooting and the cowboy yells must have taken the heart out of the bandits, I reckon, because they were in full flight now. All except El Gato. For a moment I guess he didn't miss his men, for he came straight on. Then suddenly he yanked his

272

pony back to haunches, glanced back over his shoulder. The next instant he had swung his horse around and was rapidly overtaking his fleeing men. He not only overtook them; he passed them. And they were all riding like fiends out of hell!

I heard Santiago's voice clear above the thundering of hoofs. "Come on, men, we've got them on the run now!"

We pressed in spurs and tore on. Paula was riding close by my side. Ramon wasn't far away. I didn't know how long their horses would hold up. I guess I'd been just as glad if Paula's pony had given out. I still couldn't get used to seeing a girl among all these fighting men.

I saw George Lee lift his Winchester to his shoulder. It was difficult, shooting from a galloping horse. I heard the rifle crack. Up ahead a bandit toppled from his pony and plunged down among the flying hoofs. A moment later we passed his body. It looked pretty well trampled. Our men started to shoot again. We didn't score any more hits, but the shooting did serve as a spur to the bandits' efforts to escape. We could see them beating their ponies over the heads with quirts. I had a hunch they were getting desperate. And there, far ahead of the bunch, mounted on the best horse, was El

Gato. I reckon he was realizing now that he'd bitten off more than he could chew.

22. Santiago's Revenge

We lengthened out in a long chase, Santiago riding in the lead. Rug and Lamp were close behind him. Then came the rest. Ramon's and Paula's ponies were tiring fast now. I dropped back with them, knowing I could quickly overtake the ones up in front when an occasion arose for it.

Uphill and downhill we plunged. Sometimes El Gato and his crew would get completely out of sight beyond a rise of land, but by the time we'd reached the top of the same slope we'd see them, still going. There wasn't a great deal to see, of course, just a rapidly moving cloud of dust and above the dust the sight of quirts being used right vigorously. Those quirts rose and fell . . . rose and fell. The fools were beating their horses to death.

We were gaining a trifle, but not much. The distance was too great for shooting with any accuracy now. I'd been expecting the bandits to head back toward Alzaga, but they were bearing more to the left. I don't know what El Gato had in mind, unless he hoped to reach the broken canyon country that lay over that way, in the hope of slipping off unseen. But that was still a good many miles distant, and while the quirting they were giving their ponies enabled them to keep ahead of us for a time, eventually the poor beasts would give out and we'd catch up.

Fifteen minutes slipped back of the galloping hoofs of the horses. I was still watching that cloud of dust up ahead. I saw it move swiftly up a long slope, then drop from sight on the other side. We all unconsciously put in our spurs every time those bandits rode out of sight.

Ramon yelled to me through the haze of dust that rose from our ponies' hoofs: "They can't keep it up much longer. We're due to catch 'em soon."

I nodded. I figured the firing would be hotter than ever once we'd cornered El Gato and his crew. A cornered rat always puts up a vicious fight. I glanced at Paula pounding along at my side. I was sure hoping her horse would go lame, or something. That was one time I wouldn't have stopped to wait for her.

We plunged up the long slope the bandits had covered a short time before. In front of us the dust was just commencing to settle. We were that close.

Finally we reached the top of the rise and glanced down the long gradual decline that lay ahead. Then we got the surprise of our lives. El Gato and his bandits had pulled to a halt and were sitting their droop-headed ponies with their arms high in the air. Even from this distance I could tell they were plumb agitated. At first I couldn't quite make it out.

Then suddenly it was all clear to me. El Gato and his men were caught between two fires. A quarter of a mile beyond the bandits a detachment of Mexican cavalry was coming at a swift gallop. In their khaki uniforms, and all, I hadn't at first spotted the cavalry riders against the brown hills. But they were closing in fast, and the bandits knew their time had come.

We'd all sort of slowed pace at the sight. Now Santiago signaled us to pull to a halt. We drew in and watched the proceedings from a distance. I saw the cavalry ride up and surround the bandits, then disarm them. The next moment they were forced to dismount. Even as far away as they were, I could see the reluctance in El Gato's manner as he got down from his horse. Now his last chance of escape was gone.

A few minutes later the cavalry officer in charge turned his pony and started up the

276

slope in our direction.

Santiago said, "I'd better go to meet him, I guess."

"Hadn't you better let me do that part?" I suggested.

Santiago shook his head. "No, it will be safe enough now. Ramon knows where the silver pesos are hidden, so everything will be all right. Come along if you care to though, Dale. You, too, Ramon."

He spurred his horse down the slope, and Ramon and I followed.

I was still feeling shaky about the matter, just the same, and wondering if we'd have to fight the Mex cavalry to keep them from taking Santiago with them, but everything turned out all right when Santiago met the Mexican officer. He and Santiago both gave a sudden yell of delight when they got close enough to recognize each other. It seems they were old friends. Santiago showed the papers he had from the Mexican government, and that made things all the stronger in his favor.

Then he introduced Ramon and me to the officer, who was a little roly-poly good-natured cuss: El Capitán Santandar, or some such name. I scarcely caught his moniker, I was so interested in learning what was up. It seemed the Mexican government had finally looked into El Gato's activities and decided to put a pronto stop to them. The cavalry had been sent out to round up El Gato and his bandits. El Gato was due for a court-martial. That meant he'd be stood up against a dobe wall where he'd had so many others shot down. The bandits were in for the same sort of finish, although there'd be no bothering with a court-martial where they were concerned.

It looked like the end for El Gato, all right, but it didn't turn out as planned. Santiago had other ideas. I didn't know what he was up to right off. He and the cavalry captain had reined their ponies off to one side and were talking in low, confidential tones. I looked at Ramon. He caught the thought in my mind and shrugged his shoulders. "You've got me," he admitted. "I don't know what it's all about. But you can depend on one thing — whatever Dad has in mind, it will be good."

My eyes went back to Santiago and Captain Santandar. Santiago was talking very earnestly. The captain kept shaking his head. Finally he smiled and gave a sort of dubious nod. Santiago's face lighted up like a sunrise, and he gripped the officer's hand. I knew he was plumb satisfied about something now.

Santiago looked over toward Ramon and me, then motioned us to his side. There was a sort of grim satisfaction in his face. "I've been waiting — prepared — for this for years," he said.

He climbed down from his saddle and removed the roll fastened at the cantle. He opened the roll, and I commenced to get the idea; inside were two whips. They weren't ordinary whips. I'd never seen any like 'em before. There was a stout wooden handle about fifteen inches long. Attached to that was a long braided-leather lash — it must have been twenty or twenty-five feet in length. The lash, where it joined the handle, was about an inch in thickness. From there it tapered out to a fine point at the very end, where there were some brass wires woven into it.

Santiago presented the two whips to Captain Santandar. The captain looked them over and selected one. "There seems little to choose between them, amigo." He smiled gravely.

"There isn't," Santiago replied. "They're twins — as much alike as I could have them made."

Santandar agreed. "I'll go inform El Gato Montés of your suggestion. Doubtless he will be very pleased with the idea." There was a lot of skepticism in the last words. With that the officer bowed, tucked one of the whips under his arm, and turned his horse down the hill where the bandits were being held by the soldiers.

I felt sort of let down. To me it looked like Santiago was planning to give El Gato a good flogging. Somehow it didn't seem like a real revenge. I wondered why the officer had taken one of the whips too. It occurred to me right then that, after all, I didn't know everything. Maybe there was more to this than I guessed.

I said to Santiago: "I don't quite get the idea, chief."

"It's a mystery to me too," Ramon said. There was a puzzled look in his eyes. "What's up, Dad?"

Santiago explained: "Whips such as you both just saw were in use in the Argentine — at the time El Gato Montés and I were down there. El Gato is well familiar with their use. He's something of an expert, in fact. Well, we'll see if he has forgotten any of his old skill. Captain Santandar tells me he isn't greatly perturbed over his capture. He's wiggled out of bad situations before and doubtless figures he can do the same this time. To tell the truth, I'm afraid he might. I propose to try and end the matter here and now. The captain has given his consent. I've awaited this moment for years — and I'm ready for it."

Santiago's voice was as steady as could be, but I could see he was burning up inside. Now I commenced to catch the general idea. It sort of threw me off my mental balance for a moment.

"Do you mean," I stammered, "that you — you and El Gato are going to duel with whips?"

"Exactly that," came Santiago's crisp reply. "Of course El Gato will try to kill me. If he does, Ramon — well, my papers at home are in order ———"

"Dad," Ramon broke in, "don't talk like that."

I was pretty slow on the uptake, I reckon. I still didn't get it all. I said, "You don't mean to say you can kill a man with one of those whips, do you?"

"That," Santiago said, "is to be seen."

And that's all I could get out of him. His eyes were hard now, his face determined, tight.

Ramon didn't say anything more, but he looked worried. Maybe he thought that Santiago was too old or not in fit physical condition for a duel. None of us spoke again for a time. All eyes were turned toward that group of bandits and horses and khaki-clad soldiers at the foot of the slope. Five minutes passed. There seemed to be some agitation down there. I could see Santandar talking to El Gato.

I glanced back up the slope where Paula waited with the other riders. I could see they were all puzzled, too, by what was going on. Paula started her horse toward us, then checked it again. Santiago turned and saw her just as she made the move. He motioned her on. In a moment she was at his side. He talked to her, low-voiced, for several minutes. Paula didn't say anything, but I could see her face whiten under the smudges of dirt and powder grime. Things had been moving so fast since we'd left Alzaga that I reckon she hadn't had time to do much washing.

Our attention was attracted suddenly by what sounded like a series of rifle shots. I looked down toward the soldiers and bandits and saw El Gato, stripped to the waist, trying out his whip. He was swishing it savagely back and forth, and the cracking of that brass-tipped lash sounded mighty wicked in the clear morning air. Things were commencing to look serious after all.

Santiago's eyes lighted up, and he gave a long sigh of satisfaction. "He'll fight!

Good!" That was all.

We'd clean forgotten the rest of our men waiting at the top of the hill. Now Santiago turned and motioned them on. Then he sprang into his saddle and headed down to meet El Gato. Ramon, Paula, and I were just behind him.

Santiago peeled off his upper garments on the way down the incline. Up to that time I'd been wondering if he was in condition for a fight, but after I'd seen the smooth bunches of muscle rippling across his shoulders I knew he was in his prime. El Gato was probably a few years younger than Santiago, but I doubted that the bandit would look so good.

And then when we'd arrived at the center of things I got a good look at El Gato, and my heart fell. He was in condition all right and plenty muscled up himself, with thick hair matted all over his barrellike chest. I wondered right then how I'd ever been able to give him such a beating. He was still showing the marks of that beating too. His face was cut and bruised. With a big brute like El Gato, though, those marks wouldn't make any difference in his fighting ability, so far as the duel was concerned. He happened to look my way, and I could see the hate rising in his eyes. I was glad

I wasn't within reach of his whip right then. . . .

Finally the arrangements were made. El Gato and Santiago, mounted on their horses, took up positions facing each other, about a hundred yards apart. Paula, Ramon, and I were lined up on one side with Rug Wilton, Lamp Lamonte, and the rest of our punchers. Across from us, some seventy-five yards away, were the captured bandits with the cavalry soldiers standing guard over them. A few of the soldiers were stationed behind El Gato and Santiago too. The way we were lined up, it made a sort of oblong field for the duel to be fought on.

Paula's horse was standing close to mine. She murmured, "I remember a polo match — in San Antonio — one time ——" It was the first time I'd ever heard a quiver in her voice. She couldn't go on. I couldn't think of any words, either.

A sort of tense silence settled over everything when Captain Santandar trotted his horse out to the center of the field, between the two duelists, and asked if they were ready. Then at an affirmative reply from each he drew his revolver and fired a shot in the air. That done, he swiftly loped his horse off to one side.

I can see Santiago to this day as he rode

to meet his enemy. He wasn't moving fast, but there was a sureness connected with the old war eagle's appearance that wasn't to be denied. His head with its iron-gray thatch of thick hair was high and proud. The handle of the long whip was held in his right hand, the long lash trailing along the earth as he moved.

I glanced toward El Gato, who was spurring in fast to meet his opponent. The horses drew nearer and nearer. Then as they passed I saw two muscular bare arms raise in the air, each clutching the handle of a whip. Two sinuous black lashes flashed viciously into view. . . .

Santiago had swerved his horse at just the right moment. El Gato missed his stroke, but I heard the sharp gunlike report of the lash close to Santiago's head. Then something like a savage black snake curled across El Gato's breast. It disappeared in an instant as Santiago withdrew his lash, but I was betting it drew blood. I was right. In an instant a thin crimson trickle appeared below the matted hair on El Gato's chest. Followed another and another. Then his horse had thundered past me. First blood for Santiago!

Both men whirled their mounts and came tearing into the attack again. El Gato was

maneuvering to get on his opponent's left side, but Santiago outguessed him. . . . When next they parted there was a raw red welt across El Gato's forehead. . . .

Round and round the two riders circled, the long black lashes hissing and cracking like mad. The two men would break apart an instant, then close in again, each trying to break through the other's guard. Watching the play of those whips, I guess we all missed the fact that we were witnessing some real riding. It takes a heap of skill to handle horses the way those two were doing. They'd run, dodge, side-step, retreat. It was all there: everything an expert boxer does in the way of footwork those horses were doing.

The handling of those long whips was almost too swift for the eye to follow. It was difficult to choose between the two antagonists. They were mighty evenly matched. Santiago was a mite cooler and more calculating, to my way of thinking. He was using his head every instant, while El Gato was trying to win the fight with sheer brute strength. Santiago wasn't escaping unscathed though. His body had seven or eight nasty red streaks crisscrossing it.

I didn't feel so good about that until I looked at El Gato. The big bandit was fairly

covered with blood by this time. You couldn't see the cuts clearly at all. Those curling black lashes slashed like knives. Once I glanced at Paula. Her face was white, all the color drained from it; her eyes were intent on the field before her. A strange silence lay over everything, except for the sudden staccato pounding of horses' hoofs and the savage *crack! crack! crack!* of the whip-lashes. Now and then Ramon, on my left, would jerk out a low exclamation. That was all.

Occasionally one of the duelists would turn his horse and race to the end of the field, then turn and come charging back. I'd see him come closer and closer as his opponent got under way. About the time El Gato started his stroke I'd hear Santiago's lash go singing through the air. Usually it bit deep too. El Gato was sure taking a whipping. Once Santiago's horse stumbled, and a soldier on the far side of the field let out a yell. Some expert handling by Santiago kept the horse on its feet.

That seemed to start everyone yelling. It wasn't quiet any longer. Paula had a grip on my arm that nearly paralyzed it. Ramon was swearing Spanish oaths over and over. Our cow-punchers were releasing wild cowboy yells when Santiago scored. It was the same

with the bandits across the way when El Gato got in a telling stroke.

Suddenly, as the two riders started their lashes at the same moment, the ends met in mid-air and became entangled. I saw Santiago — thinking quickly to take advantage of the situation — jerk back his arm, then the whip went sailing from El Gato's grasp. A quick flip of Santiago's wrist and the whip ends were untangled. El Gato's whip lay on the earth.

Right then Santiago had the bandit at his mercy. Instead of taking advantage of the situation he backed his horse away.

I heard one of the punchers mutter, "Hell, the chief should have finished it right then. It was his right."

I guess El Gato must have been thinking the same thing, because he hesitated a moment before riding over to get his whip. It lay only a few yards from where we were standing, and I could see he was pretty well winded when he leaned away down from his saddle and picked it up.

And then, instead of riding in to meet Santiago again, El Gato backed away to the far end of the field. Santiago was waiting for him in mid-field. The next instant the big bandit had jabbed in his spurs and came rushing to meet his adversary. The instant

with the bandits across the way when El Gato got in a telling stroke.

Suddenly, as the two riders started their lashes at the same moment, the ends met in mid-air and became entangled. I saw Santiago — thinking quickly to take advantage of the situation — jerk back his arm, then the whip went sailing from El Gato's grasp. A quick flip of Santiago's wrist and the whip ends were untangled. El Gato's whip lay on the earth.

Right then Santiago had the bandit at his mercy. Instead of taking advantage of the situation he backed his horse away.

I heard one of the punchers mutter, "Hell, the chief should have finished it right then. It was his right."

I guess El Gato must have been thinking the same thing, because he hesitated a moment before riding over to get his whip. It lay only a few yards from where we were standing, and I could see he was pretty well winded when he leaned away down from his saddle and picked it up.

And then, instead of riding in to meet Santiago again, El Gato backed away to the far end of the field. Santiago was waiting for him in mid-field. The next instant the big bandit had jabbed in his spurs and came rushing to meet his adversary. The instant

to meet his enemy. He wasn't moving fast, but there was a sureness connected with the old war eagle's appearance that wasn't to be denied. His head with its iron-gray thatch of thick hair was high and proud. The handle of the long whip was held in his right hand, the long lash trailing along the earth as he moved.

I glanced toward El Gato, who was spurring in fast to meet his opponent. The horses drew nearer and nearer. Then as they passed I saw two muscular bare arms raise in the air, each clutching the handle of a whip. Two sinuous black lashes flashed viciously into view. . . .

Santiago had swerved his horse at just the right moment. El Gato missed his stroke, but I heard the sharp gunlike report of the lash close to Santiago's head. Then something like a savage black snake curled across El Gato's breast. It disappeared in an instant as Santiago withdrew his lash, but I was betting it drew blood. I was right. In an instant a thin crimson trickle appeared below the matted hair on El Gato's chest. Followed another and another. Then his horse had thundered past me. First blood for Santiago!

Both men whirled their mounts and came tearing into the attack again. El Gato was maneuvering to get on his opponent's left side, but Santiago outguessed him. . . . When next they parted there was a raw red welt across El Gato's forehead. . . .

Round and round the two riders circled, the long black lashes hissing and cracking like mad. The two men would break apart an instant, then close in again, each trying to break through the other's guard. Watching the play of those whips, I guess we all missed the fact that we were witnessing some real riding. It takes a heap of skill to handle horses the way those two were doing. They'd run, dodge, side-step, retreat. It was all there: everything an expert boxer does in the way of footwork those horses were doing.

The handling of those long whips was almost too swift for the eye to follow. It was difficult to choose between the two antagonists. They were mighty evenly matched. Santiago was a mite cooler and more calculating, to my way of thinking. He was using his head every instant, while El Gato was trying to win the fight with sheer brute strength. Santiago wasn't escaping unscathed though. His body had seven or eight nasty red streaks crisscrossing it.

I didn't feel so good about that until I looked at El Gato. The big bandit was fairly covered with blood by this time. You couldn't see the cuts clearly at all. Those curling black lashes slashed like knives. Once I glanced at Paula. Her face was white, all the color drained from it; her eyes were intent on the field before her. A strange silence lay over everything, except for the sudden staccato pounding of horses' hoofs and the savage *crack! crack! crack!* of the whip-lashes. Now and then Ramon, on my left, would jerk out a low exclamation. That was all.

Occasionally one of the duelists would turn his horse and race to the end of the field, then turn and come charging back. I'd see him come closer and closer as hi opponent got under way. About the time E Gato started his stroke I'd hear Santiago lash go singing through the air. Usually bit deep too. El Gato was sure taking whipping. Once Santiago's horse stumbl and a soldier on the far side of the field out a yell. Some expert handling by Santi kept the horse on its feet.

That seemed to start everyone yellin wasn't quiet any longer. Paula had a gri my arm that nearly paralyzed it. Ramon swearing Spanish oaths over and over. cow-punchers were releasing wild co yells when Santiago scored. It was the

El Gato started Santiago rode to meet the rush.

For one brief instant I thought El Gato planned to ride down his opponent, but he swerved suddenly, bending low with his head shielded behind his horse's neck. For a moment I didn't realize what he was trying to do, then I saw his lash snap out, close to the ground. It curled around the front legs of Santiago's horse . . . tightened . . . then Santiago and the pony crashed to the earth!

El Gato's snarl of triumph was lost in the howl of dismay that rose from around the field. "Oh, it was foul — foul," Ramon groaned. He started forward, then checked himself.

Santiago had seen the move coming. As his horse went down he had slipped from the saddle. The dust cleared and we saw he was on his feet. Better than that: El Gato hadn't been able to check the rush of his own mount and had gone thundering past his unhorsed adversary, the whip jerked from his grip!

For the second time El Gato had lost his weapon and for the second time Santiago gave him another chance. I felt it was the last though. By the time El Gato had whirled his pony and come back Santiago had loosened the lash. His horse was un-hurt, and Santiago leaped back to the saddle the instant it was on its feet.

I saw him toss the long whip to El Gato who caught it by the handle in his right hand. But now El Gato seemed less desir-ous of forcing the fight. He backed his pony slowly away, as though wondering what to try next.

And now it was Santiago who was rushing the attack. In, out . . . in, out . . . his whiplash cracking like machine-gun fire. El Gato was helpless, dazed, before the feroc-ity of such dazzling speed.

Slowly, slowly, El Gato retreated before that merciless attack. He knew now he was a beaten man, but he put up the best defense possible, with a courage born of desperation. Some of his blows told, too, but there was nothing now could stand before Santiago's terrible onslaught. San-tiago's lash wasn't cracking so much by this time, and we knew that brass-tipped lash was finding living flesh into which to bite.

Suddenly, in a final incredible effort, El Gato jerked his horse's head around and spurred straight for Santiago in an attempt to send both horses and men crashing to the earth. It was a suicidal attempt, but El Gato must have felt it would be worth while if he could take Santiago to death with him. I held my breath . . . waiting . . . and the next instant it was all over.

Santiago had evidently been expecting a move of that sort. He swung his horse to one side, his arm raised with the speed of chain lightning; the long black lash struck through the air . . . curled viciously around El Gato's neck. The bandit leader was whipped bodily from his saddle.

As El Gato crashed to the earth I caught a sharp cracking sound. It wasn't the lash.

"God!" Rug Wilton gasped. "Santiago's broken El Gato's neck!"

23. A SILVER LINING

There isn't much more to tell. The rest of that day we took it easy and rested. The boys made a sort of tent for Paula out of their blankets, and I know she borrowed most of the water from their canteens. I borrowed the rest to shave with. I had to stand a lot of kidding from Ramon too. Santiago was some cut up, but he was feeling right comfortable and happy.

That same afternoon Captain Santandar started half of his soldiers back to Alzaga with the captured bandits. I sent my regards along to Lieutenant Estabanez and José.

Santandar was a heap curious to learn just how Paula and Ramon and I had escaped from the prison at Alzaga. I gave him a cock-and-bull story about bribing one of El Gato's soldiers to help us. I don't think he believed me, but it satisfied his conscience; if he suspected Estabanez at all he probably reasoned it had all turned out for the best anyway.

The following morning Captain Santandar, with the remainder of his cavalry troopers, started with us to the place where those silver pesos were hidden. Ramon led the way. I rode at Paula's side, and we did a heap of talking about a lot of things. Santiago treated me just the same as he did Paula and Ramon, too, and I felt mighty happy.

It was about three days' ride to where the silver was hidden. Sure, we found it all right. Vinada had stored it away in a little cave up in the hills. There was sack after sack of silver coins. I've been in a lot of banks in my time — you know, just sort of looking around — but never before had I seen so much money all stacked in one heap. The sacks were pretty rotten by the time we found them.

Another couple of days went past while Santandar sent some of his men for pack mules to carry the silver away. There was a small settlement not far from the cave, so we didn't have any trouble getting what food we needed while we were waiting for those mules. About that silver, until Santiago brought up the subject again, I'd clean forgotten I was entitled to half those pesos. I told Santiago I didn't intend to take 'em.

Santiago just laughed at me. "You're going to need 'em, son," he said, and that "son" sounded mighty good. "Sure, it's all fixed up with Santandar that half is yours, as I promised. The pack mules will be here tomorrow or next day. We'll get them packed and head back for the States. Don't worry, boy, you've earned every cent of that money. Maybe more. When we agreed on the price I didn't know you'd have to save Paula too."

"We'll forget Paula," I said shortly.

"That's more than I've ever been able to do," he said cheerfully. "And I've got a hunch you're going to be stuck the same way. That girl has a mind of her own."

I could feel my face getting red. I didn't say anything but just walked away. I heard him give a sort of chuckle as I left.

But, like I say, it was plumb comfortable waiting around for those mules to show up. I wasn't kicking any on that kind of delay. Paula and I were spending most of our time together. Starry nights out in the open, or a full moon, make a man lose his sense of proportion sometimes. I was just sort of drifting, without thinking where I was bound.

And then all of a sudden it struck me what I was doing. I knew by this time that Paula liked me a lot, but I intended that was as far as it was going. With my reputation, I simply had to see that things didn't go farther. It wasn't fair to Paula.

Well, I kept away from her the rest of that day. That night, after supper, I sat around the fire with the punchers and soldiers. I didn't make any effort to see her. I didn't know where she was. Santiago was sitting with us, talking of early adventures down in the Argentine.

A voice called me from beyond the circle of firelight. I got up and went back into the shadows. Ramon was standing there, waiting for me. I said, "What's on your mind?"

Ramon grinned and said, "I hope I'm not going to have to spend money on a shotgun."

I said again, "What's on your mind?"

"The same as on yours," he replied. "That kid sister of mine. Remember her?"

I said, "Cut out the ribbing. What about Paula?"

"About two hundred yards from here," Ramon explained, "there's a big flat rock on the crest of a hill. You ought to know where it is. Anyway, Paula says you were out there last night."

I could feel my face getting red again. I said, "Yes, I know where it is. Paula and I were watching the moon come up last night."

"I know how it is, Dale. I was young once myself. Anyway, Paula is still waiting for you tonight. She says there's another moon coming up and she wants someone to check with her and decide if it's the same one."

I started to splutter, "Aw-w ——"

Ramon said, "Sure, I know it's a bother, but go on, humor her. She's been reading love romances and has got ideas about you. I've had to put up with her all my life. I figure it's somebody else's turn now. You're elected. Maybe you can beat some sense into her head. I never could."

He gave me a push, and I started out with his laugh ringing in my ears. I was commencing to get sort of mad. Maybe Paula did need somebody to lay the law down to her. That was the trouble with her. She had romantical notions. Once she was back at the university she'd forget all about me. That's the way it should be.

I found her waiting on the rock for me. I sat down beside her. There were a lot of stars hanging low overhead. It wasn't time for the moon to come up yet. She sort of snuggled a little closer to me and put a hand on one of mine. I jerked it away.

I said, "Now look here, Paula. You've been getting ideas and ——"

"Sure I have," she admitted. "We've wasted time. There's no sense our waiting until we reach the States to get married. After we start home we'll stop at the first good-sized town and ——"

"What!" I half yelled. "Say, have you gone crazy?"

"Shut up," she said, "I'm doing the talking."

"I won't shut up," I snapped at her. "Ramon said you were getting ideas and ——"

"Ramon always said I was a hussy too. Maybe I am. But if you won't do the proposing I'll have to."

Mister, she sure had me down for the count. I was gasping for air while she out-talked me. Finally I got a word in edgewise: "Look, Paula, it all sounds very nice, but it can't be. I've been a bandit most of my life and ——"

"That's all right with me," she cut in. "If you don't want to give up your work I'll go along and help you. Maybe we can make twice as much as you did alone."

I said, "Now I know you're crazy."

"I've already admitted that. But from now on you can't lose me. Understand?"

She sure had me pawing at the atmosphere. After a time I did get her to the point where she'd talk seriously. "Look," I told her, "this is all a very nice dream, but if you married me it simply wouldn't work out. You know the cloud I'm under ——"

"There's an old saying to the effect that every cloud has a silver lining, Dale. Well, you've got your share of the silver and ——"

"I'm not going to take it."

"Oh yes, you are. You're going to need it to fix yourself up for the things you've done in the past. Besides, we've got to have something to live on."

"How are we going to fix what I've done in the past?" I asked her.

Then she told me something her father hadn't even mentioned. Santiago had got busy and pulled a lot of wires after that night at the Golden Cactus. It seemed he was mighty close to a couple of governors in whose states I'd operated in the past. Anyway, with his pull Santiago fixed it so I was to be pardoned for my crimes on condition I returned the money I'd lifted. And as

Paula pointed out, "Dale, your share of the silver will more than take care of that."

So there you are. I couldn't hold out any longer. And Paula wasn't giving me time to think straight. No getting away from it; there wasn't anyone else for either of us. I felt myself slipping fast. All the barriers I erected were blasted down as fast as I put them up. Paula had the answer to everything that night, except one thing. She said finally, "Look, I've done the proposing. Aren't you going to take me in your arms and kiss me?"

I answered that one myself. . . .

We hope you have enjoyed this Large Print book. Other Thorndike, Wheeler, and Chivers Press Large Print books are available at your library or directly from the publishers.

For information about current and upcoming titles, please call or write, without obligation, to:

Publisher
Thorndike Press
295 Kennedy Memorial Drive
Waterville, ME 04901
Tel. (800) 223-1244

or visit our Web site at:

www.gale.com/thorndike
www.gale.com/wheeler

OR

Chivers Large Print
published by BBC Audiobooks Ltd
St James House, The Square
Lower Bristol Road
Bath BA2 3SB
England
Tel. +44(0) 800 136919
email: bbcaudiobooks@bbc.co.uk
www.bbcaudiobooks.co.uk

All our Large Print titles are designed for easy reading, and all our books are made to last.